YOUR HUSBAND'S CHEATING ON US 3

MZ. BIGGS

Shan Presents, LLC

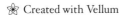 Created with Vellum

SUBSCRIBE

Text Shan to 22828 to stay up to date with new releases, sneak peeks, contest, and more...

Text SPROMANCE to 22828 to stay up to date on new releases, plus get information on contests, sneak peeks, and more!

ACKNOWLEDGMENTS

As always, I have to thank God for placing me where he thought I should be. This road is not easy to travel, but I'm a fighter. With His will, all things are done.

This book was the very first series that I've ever written. The initial title was See What Had Happened Was: A Contemporary Love Story. While this is a re-release, it is my absolute favorite series. There were times where I felt defeated and wanted to give up. I didn't. It's because of the great people who took the time to follow me through this journey. There was a time when I didn't think my book three was going to be published. However, it all worked out. I have to thank my publisher, Shan, for continuing to believe in me.

Brooklyn Hughes, thank you again for allowing me to use you on my book cover.

Thanks again to my family, friends, and supporters. You motivate me to continue on this journey. I'm moving full speed ahead. Please remember to leave a review and let me know what you think. Thanks in advance.

-Mz. Biggs

"If you can't fly, then run. If you can't run, then walk. If you can't walk, then crawl. But whatever you do, you have to keep moving forward."

-Martin Luther King Jr.

It's amazing how you'll never know who or what is placed in your life to serve as motivation for you. From the time I decided to get my feet wet, I spoke with a friend about what I wanted to do and he continuously pushed me to go for it. When I was tired, felt like giving up, wanted to throw my hands up in defeat, he reminded me that if it was something I truly wanted, I would see it as an opportunity and not make excuses. Failure was not an option. Even when you were down, you still listened to me vent or allowed me to send you the paper copies of my book so you could provide me with your feedback. I can't thank you enough for how much of a friend and supporter you have been for me. I dedicate this book to you, Everett Williams. I'm glad you're back!

CHECK OUT MY OTHER GREAT BOOKS:

See What Had Happened Was: A Contemporary Love Story (Book 1-3)
My First Taste of A Bad Boy (1-3)
Dirty South: A Dope Boy Love Story
Falling for A Dope Boy (1-3)
Feenin' For That Thug Lovin (1-3)
Jaxson and Giah: An Undeniable Love (1-2)
Finding My Rib: A Complicated Love Story
In Love With My Cuddy Buddy (1-2)
This Book is a Collaboration with Author Tyanna

Want to connect with me? Here's how:

email: authoress.mz.biggs@gmail.com
Twitter: @mz_biggz
Instagram: mz.biggs
Goodreads: Mz. Biggs
Facebook: https://www.facebook.com/authoress.biggs
Author Page: https://www.facebook.com/MzBiggs3/

Look for my Reading Group on Facebook: Mz. Biggs Reading Group

WHERE WE LEFT OFF...

Cameron

Since everything has been going wrong with me, I couldn't stomach the thought of going to work. It would be too awkward for me and that was something I wasn't prepared for, so I took some time off.

As I laid in bed, I thought about all the stuff Darnell had going on with him. He was my boy at one point, but now he was tripping behind some bitch. To me, she wasn't worth all the trouble, but I can understand loving someone and them not returning the feeling.

"Cameron, don't you hear me calling you?" Afreeca shouted while popping me on the leg with a wet towel trying to get my attention.

"Yeah, I'm listening to you, hell. What do you want?" I snapped back at her. She was working my last nerve with all of her nagging.

"Look, we have got to get a good plan in motion because I'm tired of playing games with these two. You promised me you would help me get Darnell. In order for that to happen, we have to get that Kat bitch out the picture. Even if we have to kill her, I don't care," she fretted.

If only she knew what she'd gotten herself into, she would get out of my face quick, but I won't let her in on my real plans until after I've had all the fun I planned on having. At the end of the day, the only one who would be coming out on top of all of this would be me.

Nobody knows that for a while, I've had underlying feelings towards men. Looking at me, there was no way anyone could tell that I was gay. Actually, I'm bi-sexual, but none of that really matters to me. That worked in my favor because I never had to worry about someone discriminating against me.

When I met Darnell, there was something about him that caught my eye. I had to give it to him, he commanded attention. There was no way he could be in your presence and you not be drawn to him. It took everything in me to keep my manhood from pushing a hole in my pants each time I saw him.

I'd just been laid off from my previous job and didn't know what to do. I saw the posting for a Program Specialist, so I applied. When I applied for the position, it took about a month to get called in for an interview.

The day I walked into the building, I was in awe at how big it was and the amount of traffic going in and out of the building. I can say that the security was on point. Nobody was getting in without showing proper credentials.

Walking up to the receptionist, I informed her that I had an interview. She gave me a funny look like she had a problem with me. Luckily for her, I was there to interview so I had to bite my tongue and not say what I really wanted to say to her ass.

She told me to sit down and someone would be out to get me shortly. When I finally got to the back, I realized it was a mock interview. There were about 8 people sitting in on my interview, including Darnell.

Sitting down, I was able to make eye contact with him. There was a slight sparkle in his eye, and when he smiled, I could've melted at how beautiful his teeth were. There's something about a man with beautiful teeth that could instantly get my shit hard. I almost thought I was going to flip the table over with how quick my dick stood up.

I breezed through my interview and was called a week later and offered the job. I didn't get to start until about two months after that because of how drastic the hiring process was.

The day I finally reported to work, Nell was the person I was assigned to shadow. I watched his every move. To him, I was making sure I was catching on to what the job entailed, but I was really watching to see if I would be able to see a dick print in his pants.

About four months of me working there, Darnell and I ended up working late, trying to get an assignment done. He started rubbing his neck and made a comment about having a crook in it. I went over to him and started massaging around his shoulders and neck.

At first, he appeared to be uncomfortable and was jumpy each time I touched him. But the more I rubbed on him, the more I noticed his body loosen up. When I noticed him closing his eyes, I tiptoed over to the door and locked it.

Moving back over to Darnell, I pulled his chair back from his desk. Luckily it was on wheels because I don't think I ever would've got the chair to move otherwise.

Waiting until I thought he was in a deep sleep, I eased down to my knees in front of him after pushing his legs apart. Slowly unzipping his pants, I pulled his rod through the hole in his boxers. My eyes bulged when I noticed how big it was.

Using my hands, I started stroking his one-eyed monster wanting to wake it up. Darnell started to moan although it could barely be heard. Gently wrapping my mouth around his dick, I moved it up and down being sure to use my tongue to give his head special attention.

"Oh bae, damn baby, that feels good!" Slanting my eyes, I looked up at him with a burning desire to bite his ass. I couldn't believe he'd just called me another woman's name. It was at that time I was determined to show him who could please him.

Knowing that he was in a deep dream, I continued slobbering on his meat getting it nice and wet while I slowly undid my pants and slid them down to my knees. Positioning myself into a squat in front of him, I was able to slide my pants all the way off.

Spitting on my hand, I rubbed my anus to get it good and wet while I continued to slob on his knob. Raising up, I turned around and eased down on top of him. Feeling his body tense up behind me only turned me on more.

Squeezing my cheeks together, I began to go faster and faster. While riding him, I started to stroke my own dick. It was feeling so good to me, until he opened his eyes and realized what he was doing. He pushed me off him and I could see the disgust in his eyes.

"Man, what the fuck are you doing?" He yelled at me.

"You were enjoying it. Just let it happen," I responded to him.

"Aye Cameron, I'm not gay. This shouldn't have happened. This is bullshit!"

He screamed as he lunged towards me. Damn, I never thought that would happen. I was making him feel good, so why would he attack me?

He grabbed me around my neck and rammed me against the wall. I could feel my knees getting weak and my body wanting to collapse as he started bashing my head against the wall.

Trying to plead with him I asked him to let me explain. He let me go so I thought that was his way of giving me a chance to explain. I should've known better than that because when I was finally able to compose myself, I heard a slamming noise followed by a clicking sound.

Looking up at him, I could see him pointing a gun at my head. "Please Darnell, let me explain!" I begged him to let me talk to him. I even dropped to my knees and moved my hands up to my mouth like I was praying. Hell, I really was praying. Praying that nigga didn't splatter my brains all over the wall.

Like a raging bull, his nostrils kept flaring in and out as he was catching his breath and his body was trembling. The expression on his face was one of hate!

"I'm sorry, Darnell. See what had happened was, I have an interest in men and from the time I saw you, I've wanted you. This was the only opportunity I had to see if you would go for it. I heard you moaning, so I know that you had to have liked it a little," I pleaded as I started to tear up.

I continued begging and pleading with him until I noticed him becoming at ease. He began pacing back and forth contemplating what his next move would be, I assumed.

Noticing that his pants and boxers were now to his knees, I looked up at Darnell. He briskly walked over to me, turned me facing the wall and rammed his dick back inside of me without checking to see if I was ready for entry.

I can remember being sore for weeks after my first encounter with him. He ignored me for a while after that. It wasn't until we were given another assignment together that he started back talking to me.

That was when he gave me my nickname, bae. From that day on, Darnell didn't seem to care about my feelings at all, but from the first time we were together, I managed to get him in the bed several times after that. It wasn't until that Kat bitch came into the picture that he really started to ignore me, unless it was something work-related.

Now, I was going to have to get rid of her and Afreeca who I initially made hook up with him. I had her believing that I could get them together when I really wanted to get his mind off Kat. Not only do I have one bitch to get rid of, now I have two.

Afreeca

"Bitch, you hear me talking to you?" I probed Cameron. It looked like I was snapping him out of some type of daydream or something.

"I hear your loud ass. Gone somewhere with that shit. I told you things would happen in due time."

I was starting to become restless with him. He told me that he had a co-worker he wanted to introduce me to; he thought that we would be a great match. On the first night that I met him, I really enjoyed our conversation.

While Darnell became super drunk and I was a little tipsy, Cameron drove us back to Darnell's house. He didn't know it, but Cameron and I both had a good time with him that night.

Normally, I would run from a brother that was on the down low, but I didn't think he was really that way. I believe he was more so taking advantage of an opportunity that was presented to him to get his dick wet.

Cameron promised me that he would figure out how to get Darnell and me together, but that has yet to happen. He even had me texting him like I'm pregnant to see if he would try to be there for his child.

The only dilemma with that was Cameron having me text him without revealing who I was. That's the dumbest shit ever, if you ask me.

All of the ideas he'd thrown out there to come out ahead of the game has backfired on us. We've followed him, vandalized shit, had Kateshia's husband blamed for some shit; pretty much you name it, we've done it.

Some people may say we were being petty, but I highly doubt it. I was out to get my man by any means necessary.

If ole dumbass Cameron thinks he's going to outsmart me by getting Darnell on his own, then he isn't playing with a full deck because I'm going to make this shit do what it do until I get what I came for. He's going to end up making me hit his ass so hard on the top of the head that I cause him to split another asshole.

Right now, all I can do is sit back and wait for our last and final plan to work...

To Be Continued......

K *ateshia*
"Let me out, let me out now!" I frantically screamed as I scavenged around what appeared to be a wooden box that I was in. It was so dark and cold in there that I could feel my body shivering out of control. Hastily searching around for something to cover my bare body, I was scared out of my mind. I've never been so scared in my life.

From all the kicking, screaming, and punching I was doing, you would've thought someone would've heard me by now and came to rescue me. Nobody came. The only thing I felt coming was a panic attack.

Gradually inhaling and exhaling long, deep breaths, I attempted to calm myself down. Suddenly, I could feel a warm liquid begin to trickle down my leg. I can't believe I was pissing on myself.

Not knowing how much longer I would be in that box, I moved my hand between my legs as quickly as possible to catch some of my urine. Easing my hand up to my mouth, I used my other hand to hold the tip of my nose as I moved as slow as a snail, drinking what little urine I was able to catch.

I attempted to hold my nostrils as tight as I could to prevent from smelling the urine while I drank it. Just my luck, a swift breeze flowed through the box, causing me to flinch as the scent attacked the small openings in my nostrils. I couldn't believe what I was doing, but hell, it was all about survival at that point.

"Please help me! Somebody get me out of here; I can't breathe!" I continuously begged for help, but to no avail. *What the hell was going on? How did I get here?* Multiple thoughts flourished in my mind as I tried to recall the events that led to me being held captive. There had to be something significant I could remember that would help me get out of there alive. There just had to be!

Closing my eyes, I allowed my thoughts to consume me further. Only that time, the thoughts were of the last twenty-four hours before waking up in this dark space. I knew I'd been in there for a while, but I just couldn't pinpoint exactly how long it had been.

This had Tavares's name written all over it. I mean, who else would do some shit like this to me? And where the hell was Darnell's ass? I knew damn well he didn't gain enough strength back, then dip his ass out the house, leaving me to fend for myself, when the main reason I stayed in the house was to rescue his ass.

See, the way my mind is set up at the moment, no one was safe from feeling my wrath. If I got out of there alive, whoever did that to me would have hell to pay. Nobody had seen the last of me.

Ha ha ha ha ha…

I could hear someone uncontrollably laughing as they proceeded to move closer to me.

"Dear Sweet Kat, you're even more beautiful in person. And to know that you taste even sweeter almost made my heart skip a beat," I could hear an evil voice proclaim. What the hell did they mean about me tasting sweet? What the hell was wrong with their voice? I could tell they were using some type of voice box, so I was unable to make out who it could have possibly been.

"Who are you? What do you want from me?" I yelled out, hoping I would be able to get even a partial answer.

"You don't ask the questions here; I do! It seems to me that you have yourself in a bad situation, granting you only a tiny amount of space to maneuver your way out of this." They continued to laugh, but I didn't find any of this shit to be funny.

"Well, can you at least tell me where I am?" I asked as calmly as possible.

"You're inside of a box. You haven't been smart enough to figure that out yet? Nooo... not Perfect Patty! Something finally went over your perfect little head?" They humorously teased, as if they were being paid to be a comedian.

"Yeah, we all can't be a genius like you! Do you know who my husband is?" I despairingly shouted, praying that would scare them a little if Tavares wasn't behind this.

"Bitch please; we all know who your 'soon-to-be' ex-husband is. We also know that he would kill you himself if he could find you."

Bingo! The fire that was in their voice when they spat their response let me know that they were connected to Tavares in some type of way. It surely had to be a broad going through all of that trouble trying to get rid of me.

"Let me guess, you're one of the many obstacles he's tackled, so you kidnapped me and are planning to kill me, so you can have him for yourself? He must've been slanging major dick your way to have you acting loopy as hell," I uttered at her, really getting more agitated at the high level of bullshit.

The rage in her voice really let me know it was a woman. Then, the fact that I started to piss her off so much that she forgot to use her voice box further proved me right. My only goal now was to make her mad enough to want to pull me out this box and put her hands on me. Yeah, that's exactly what I needed her to do and I was more than prepared to beat that ass.

"What the hell are you even talking about? Who is he and who are you calling a herd? In case you haven't figured it out yet, you are in no position to crack jokes, make demands, or ask all these damn questions," she angrily retorted.

"Tavares! You know exactly who I'm talking about. And who said anything about a herd? I said hurdle. Are you one of his little bitches? Yeah, I bet you are. Well, guess what sweetie, he can go out there and screw you until your brains fall out. Hell, he can screw everyone in the state of New York, but guess who he always comes back home to boo-boo?" Crossing my fingers, I was hoping that I was saying enough to push all the right buttons to get her to snap.

Just then, I could feel the box starting to move. I'm not sure if she was trying to open it or not, but if she was planning to kill me anyways, I was going to give her more than enough reason to do so. I was not going down without a fight. I was going to taunt the hell out of her and get some type of pleasure from it before I made my appearance at the 'Pearly Gates'.

"So, all I want to know is are you BIG mad or nah? I'm sure it must piss you off knowing that you were the side dish to his main course. Even when I was giving him away, he still tried to come back. Face it dear, you will always be a second choice, if not a third or fourth!"

"What the hell do you mean third or fourth? I'm nobody's second choice." I could just feel her about to snap and I was ready for her ass.

"See, that's where you're wrong. You're so busy trying to harm me that you fail to see the bigger picture. Yeah, he cheated on me with you, but he cheated on you with my sister and God only knows who else. You're just an option, my dear; he will never make you a priority."

That must've been the straw that broke the camel's back. The next thing I knew, the box began to rock irrepressibly until it fell over and I rolled out. Turning around to face my captor, I couldn't believe who was staring me in my face.

T 2

Tavares

After a week of being in the hospital, I was glad to finally be returning home. The whole time I was in there, the police were crawling in and out of my room, questioning me about the night Kat disappeared. I did whatever I could to keep my story straight.

The media was eating up the fact that a prominent attorney, such as myself, was attacked along with his wife by her estranged ex-boyfriend, and now, his wife and her ex were both missing. You've got to admit that I was smart as hell, coming up with that story so quick. There was no way I was going to jail fucking with Kat, so I was going to let this play out for as long as I could. In the meantime, I also knew I was going to have to find both Kat and Darnell before the police did.

"Excuse me Mr. Jordan; are you ready to make a statement?" Officer Coleman calmly asked me with a sour expression on her face.

"Yeah, give me a few more minutes to get my thoughts together. I'm used to talking to the press, but this time hits close to home and I don't want to say anything that will throw up any red flags," I blurted out without thinking. "I mean, they already think my story sounds fishy, due to our recent history, so I don't want people thinking I harmed my wife," I hurriedly spoke, trying to recover from my last statement.

Rolling her eyes at me, I could tell that she already had me pegged as being guilty before I even faced a jury. Hell, I haven't even been arrested for anything, so I was waiting for her moley faced ass to say the wrong thing to me. She stayed walking around looking like she was eating on a damn sour patch kid. Frankly, I was tired of looking at her ass.

"Let's move this along, Mr. Jordan; some of us do have to actually be out there looking for Mrs. Jordan," she snapped at me like she wanted to bite my head off. Hell, I was looking for Kat's ass too. Just not for the same reasons they were. I wanted her more than people knew it.

"I'm ready. Let's just get this over with, so you can get the hell out of my face." I had already had more than enough of her and was not afraid to let her know.

Officer Coleman slowly walked towards me with a wicked grin on her face. "I don't like you either. Niggas like you are why we are given a bad name as black people. I know that you had something to do with this, and I'm going to make sure you go down for her disappearance, if I have to work day and night for it to happen.

"So, take your Uncle Tom ass out there to put on a show for these other people, but know that I will be watching your every move. You will pay for what you did and when that time comes, I will be the first one to buy you your soap on a rope," she happily stated before walking away.

I knew then that I was going to have to work faster to find Kat's ass. She was causing me more problems than she was worth. The look in Officer Coleman's eyes let me know that she meant business, but her ass wouldn't get the chance to use me to advance her career, which I'm sure was the real reason she was pushing to solve this case.

Making my way out my front door to my porch, I got behind the big wooden podium that was waiting for me. Lights flashed at what appeared to be hundreds of people covering my front lawn, waiting to hear my speech. Kat's parents walked up beside me as we prepared to address the eagerly awaiting crowd.

Tap... Tap...

I hit the mic to make sure it was on. Silence fell down on me as it became quiet enough to hear a pin drop. I flipped through my note cards looking for where to begin my speech. Nervousness took complete control over my body as I tried to force tears to drain from my eyes. I knew I needed to be as convincing as I possibly could be.

"First, let me thank everyone for coming out to show support while I search for my wife." I paused to hold up a picture of Kat and me. I could feel her mother softly place her hand into mine. Her father just stood there giving me a cold stare.

"Kat and I have been together for a very long time and she is undoubtedly the love of my life. It saddens me that someone would invade our home and take her away from me. Please return her to me safely. If you are asking for money, then let me know how much. I will give anything to have my wife back home with me."

"Mr. Jordan, it has come to our attention that you and your wife were recently in court due to her filing for a divorce from you. How do we know you aren't behind her disappearance?" a redheaded, freckled-faced reporter asked me.

I wanted desperately to tell his white ass to place his lips on the crack of my ass. Instead, I simply stated, "Well, if you would've continued your research, then you would know that she returned back home and we were working on our marriage." That shut his Carrot Top looking ass up.

"I would like to say that I am sorry that such a tragic event has just happened to you. Can you give us any insight as to what happened that night up until the time of her disappearance?" Another reported inquired. She did at least try to show some form of sympathy, but she was still being nosey as hell.

"I can tell you exactly what happened. Tavares is putting on a show for y'all to show pity towards him. That bastard killed my sister! She's not missing; she's dead!" Lateshia furiously exclaimed, popping out of nowhere while making her way through the crowd to stand beside her parents and I. Oh, this bitch was definitely going to be seeing me when this shit was over....

❧ 3 ❧

Lateshia

"You say she's your sister; how was your relationship with her?" a reporter asked me, getting a little too personal. Why the hell did they need to know how my relationship was with my sister?

"That's neither here nor there. The only thing that matters right now is that my sister is missing and Tavares was the last person to see her alive. She tried to get away from him. He pushed and pushed until she came back to this hellhole that he likes to call a house. I know my sister would never willingly return to him. Do some research and find out why she really returned, and I'm sure you will see like me, that some shady shit had to have gone down."

After giving my statement, I walked over to my mother and whispered in her ear that I urgently needed to talk to her. I was feeling like a pressure cooker about to pop my top, so I needed to talk to someone fast.

My mother nodded her head, letting me know she heard me, but I knew it would have to wait until after the press conference was over. We stood out there another ten minutes before one of the detectives went to the podium to finish up the press conference while my parents, Tavares, and I went inside the house he once shared with my sister.

It was awkward being back in that house after everything that went down between Tavares and I the last time I was there. Just as I was beginning to think about that dreaded night, I could hear Tavares begin to go on and on about something.

"Lateshia, what in the hell would possess you to bring your ass to the podium accusing me of hurting Kat? You know damn well I loved her!"

"Loved, huh? Are you saying that she is dead? Is that the reason you're speaking in past tense?" He stood there looking dumbfounded. Yeah, he could play that innocent shit with my parents, but I knew him on a deeper level, so I knew he wasn't about shit. "Tavares, where is my sister? She probably came back, realized this wasn't what she wanted, and tried to leave again. I'm sure once she tried to leave, your ass done whatever you could to stop her, even if you had to kill her."

Saying more than I probably should've, Tavares charged at me and had me pinned against the wall before I knew it.

"Let me tell you this, I didn't kill my wife and I had nothing to do with her disappearance. What you will not do is fuck up my life with your accusations. Maybe they need to be looking at you to see where she is. It's not like your ass wasn't jealous of her. And I know for a fact that your ass wanted her life."

He continued to go on and on about how worthless I was and my jealousy issues with my sister. I did everything that I could to stop the tears from flowing down my face. It was unreal how bad he was making me feel. How the hell could he try to turn this shit around on me when he was the last one to see her alive?

So many questions were going through my head, but I knew better than to ask his ass any one of those questions; especially not while he had me hemmed up in that corner.

"Tavares, what in the world are you doing? I've never seen this side of you before," my mother finally stepped up to say. I could see her out the corner of my eyes beginning to tear up, which was something I wasn't about to do. There was no way I was going to give him the privilege of seeing me shed another tear because of him.

"I'm trying to be as calm as I can about everything that's going on, but if you don't get your damn hands off my daughter, there will be two bodies missing. No, I take that back. One will still be missing, but the other one will be easily found, only it will be stinkin' when it is," my father sternly spat through clenched teeth, as he began to walk up on Tavares.

My mother slid in front of him, blocking his path to Tavares as he quickly removed his hand from my throat and backed away from me. His eyes were red and sleek. I could see then, that he really didn't know where Kat was. But, there was no way I could get past the feeling that he had done something to her. I knew he did.

Rubbing my neck, I could only try to think of a way to get Tavares to trust me enough to tell me what really went down the last time he saw my sister.

"Tavares, look, maybe I was out of line, but there are some things that aren't adding up. You're an attorney, a damn good one at that. Think of all the cases you've tried. If someone would've come at you with the same story you are presenting to us and they had the same history that you and my sister have, what would you think?"

"Lat, I know that it doesn't seem right, but I'm telling you I have nothing to do with her disappearance."

"Then, why don't you tell us what happened the last time you saw her? There has to be something that you're missing that could be a big clue," my mother curiously probed.

"Kat and I were upstairs making love when I heard a loud noise downstairs. I told her to stay up there while I ran down the stairs to see what was going on. Next thing I know, I was being rushed from behind. Looking up at the mirror, I could see it was Darnell behind me, so I began to fight him trying to get the upper hand. He carried too much strength for me, so there was really nothing I could do. He kicked me down the stairs into the basement.

"I didn't see him or Kat anymore after that. I remember being taken to the hospital where I've been for the last week because of all of this mess. So, like I said, I don't know where Kat is," Tavares detailed, trying to convince us to believe his story. No matter how many times he could've laid it out there to me, there was no way I could believe him.

"I'm sorry, but this just isn't adding up. We both know that Kat didn't want to be here and she definitely wouldn't be in here making love to you."

"Bitch, you don't know shit. She realized that she loved me and our home is where her heart was, so she surely did get the hell in bed with me. I smashed the hell out of that pussy. You remember how I used to do yours, right?" He boasted, loud enough for my parents to hear him and realize what he said.

He appeared as though he didn't care that he'd just revealed our big secret to my parents. My mother gasped for air and my father glared at me with a shocked look on his face.

"What the hell did you just say?" My father solicited, pretty much demanding a response from him.

"Kat didn't tell you?" Tavares worriedly replied.

"Tell us what?" My mother queried, also wanting answers.

"Mom and Dad, we will talk about this later. Right now, we have to worry about where Kat is and how we can bring her back home safely," I interjected, hoping they would remember that this was about Kat and not me and the stupid mistake I made.

"No, we will talk about this shit now. You two are keeping something from us and we want to know what the hell you're talking about and I mean right the hell now!" my father demanded, enraged at what he knew he was about to hear.

"Lateshia and I had an affair a while back. It was a stupid mistake and I've regretted it since the day it has happened. Please know that I do love Kat and hate that all of this has gone on. I especially hate that you all have to deal with a daughter being missing and learning that your other daughter is a slu-!"

My father didn't give him enough time to finish his statement before he attacked him. My mother didn't do anything to try to stop the attack from happening this time. Glad to see my parents finally standing up to protect me. I was horrified at what Tavares could do to my father. Not missing a beat, I jumped in to help my father out. With both of us hot on his ass, he had no choice, but to fall to the floor. Pushing me out the way, my father pulled Tavares up to his feet. For a brief moment, I could hear material from his shirt ripping as my father was pulling him up by the top of it. Looking at his high-priced shirt that was now torn, Tavares swung at my father, causing my father to stumble backward, dodging the blow.

Seeing everything take place before my eyes further stunned me. The nerve of Tavares to try to put his hands on my father and think I would allow him to get away with it. I hastily hopped on his back and began swinging my hands hysterically, sending blow after blow to his head. If it were up to me, I would've bashed his brains out. While I was tearing his ass up from the back, my father began sending jolts to his stomach with his fists.

"Stop this right now!" my mother hollered out in terror. You would've thought someone was trying to kill her the way she was bawling out. Taking initiative to gain control of what was going on, my mother walked over and began trying to pull us apart. When I realized what she was doing, I moved away from the fight to avoid hitting her.

Still going toe to toe, I watched on as my mother attempted to get Tavares and my father apart. After another ten minutes of them fighting, she was finally able to get them to stop their feuding. But, just looking at them, it was clear to see they were more than ready to pounce on each other again at any given moment.

4

Darnell

 Kat tried her best to get me out of the basement, but my body weight was too much for her to carry. Taking my time to build my strength back up, I managed to make it up the stairs and in the kitchen without anyone seeing me.

 Not having enough strength to put up a fight with anyone, I waited things out before trying to make an escape. When I heard the commotion going on in the basement, I took my time going up the next set of steps hoping to hide out in a vacant bedroom. I could hear the sirens from a distance as I was making my way up the stairs.

 Dipping inside the master bedroom, I managed to grab my clothes. I rushed to put them on as I said a silent prayer that I would be able to make it out of there before the police arrived. Being in a situation like that definitely wouldn't look good for my career.

 Finally getting myself dressed, I forced myself to tiptoe back down the stairs, slowly passing by the basement door trying to see if there was any movement down there. Peeking down into the basement, I could see Kat down there handling business with Tavares. Feeling as if the police were close by and she had the upper hand of the situation, I made a U-turn and vaulted out the front door towards my car.

Without giving things a second thought, I crank my car and got the hell out of dodge. I'd just have to catch up with Kat later to find out what happened to Tavares. I just hoped I was making the right decision as I drove off without bothering to look back.

Watching the ceiling fan rotate clockwise above my head, I laid in the bed, staring at what appeared to be a wet spot in the ceiling. There I was, in a hotel, allowing my body to occupy the warm, soft, cozy queen size bed; not knowing what was up with my queen.

It'd been a week since I'd seen or talked to Kat, which wasn't like her. She always kept in constant contact with me. It made me so sick, that I couldn't eat and I was barely sleeping. I turned my phone off as soon as I got to the hotel, but turned it back on yesterday, just in case she called. Yet, I heard nothing from her or anyone else.

Feeling myself becoming nauseous, I hurried out of the bed, making it to the bathroom with enough time to lean over the toilet. Thinking I was about to vomit, the only thing I could see coming up was a clear liquid. My head was hurting, I had bags under my eyes, and I wasn't thinking straight. I wouldn't even turn the TV on, for fear that I would see Kat on there for murdering Tavares.

Finding enough courage to get myself out of the room, I fumbled through the pile of clothes inhibiting the floor, causing them to be launched further across the room. Tossing on a pair of jogging pants and my graphic "Straight Outta Moss Point" t-shirt, I didn't bother to put on any boxers or socks, for that matter. I planned to grab a newspaper, something to eat, and return back to the room.

Ring.... Ring...

My phone began to ring, causing me to stop in my tracks. Scavenging around the room trying to locate my phone, I was praying it was Kat on the other end. Discovering it under some trash in the corner of the room, I picked up the phone, only to notice that the face flashing across my screen belonged to Cameron. I didn't want to be bothered by him, but I figured he would only keep calling me back if I didn't go ahead and answer.

"*Sup?*" I irritably asked. I really hoped he could see that I didn't want to be bothered and make the conversation short and simple.

"*Hey boo! How's everything going with you? I haven't heard from you and I wanted to make sure everything was good with you. Where are you?"* Now, I'm no genius, but I knew he was up to something.

Deciding to play it cool, I simply stated, *"I've been around. I haven't heard from Kat, so I'm trying to wait around and make sure she's good before I leave town."*

"What do you mean make sure she's good? Do you know where she is? Her face has been plastered all over the news as a missing person."

"Wait... what did you just say? What do you mean she's missing?" I sat there with my mouth wide open. You would've thought I needed to use my hands to press my lips back together.

"Yeah, she's been missing for like a week. You're listed as a suspect in her disappearance. They've sent officers up here looking for you and everything. And the fact that no one has seen you or been able to get in contact with you doesn't look good for you either," he informed me. The more he talked, the more I was feeling sick to my stomach again.

My head instantly started to throb from all the information he had given me. What the hell had Kat gotten me into? Looking for her to rekindle what we had in high school turned out to be the worse decision I've ever made.

After hearing the information Cameron gave me, I hung the phone up while he was still talking. I knew he would be mad, but I didn't care. If what he was saying was true, I knew I'd either have to go to the police or go on the run.

Being that Tavares was as ruthless as Kat said he was, I knew I'd need to be prepared before showing up at the police station. Picking up my phone, I attempted to reach Kat one more time. When I couldn't get an answer from her, I called the next best person...my attorney.

5

*K*ateshia
Staring my capturer in the face, I knew I had seen the woman standing in front of me somewhere before, but I couldn't place where I saw her at. She stood before me looking at me, as if she was ready to attack at any moment. She was gawking at me like a hawk does its prey.

"What do you want from me?" I curiously asked, making sure not to take my eyes off her. There was no way I would allow her to surprise me with a sneak attack.

"Because of you, I can't be happy with the man I truly want. With you out of the picture, I'll be there to pick up the pieces and he'll have no choice, but to see how much he loves me too."

"I'm telling you that I don't want Tavares. I don't know how many times I can tell people that. He means nothing to me. All he's done was lie to me, cheat on me, and beat me. If that's what you call love, I don't want it," I frenziedly screamed at her, letting her know that I meant what I was saying.

"Yeah, you say that now, but I know that's only because you're trying to save your own life. What happened to all that big shit you were talking when I had you confined inside that box? Remember, I will always be second when it comes to you?" she replied, spitting back some of the stuff I'd said just to piss her off.

"I was only telling you that to make you mad. I was hoping you would get angry enough to let me out of that box. I seriously don't want Tavares. I filed for divorce; he stalked me. I left him, the house, and everything in it; he forced me to return. We can call him now and I will have him confirm everything that I'm telling you."

"Do you really think I'm about to fall for that? Why would I call him only for you to tell him where you are or that I have you?"

"I promise I won't say anything. I'm just hoping that once you hear him tell you that I don't want him and that he's been the one pursuing me, then maybe you'll let me go."

"This is what you're failing to realize. I'm not letting you go, even if he tells me that he's coming after you. The fact still remains that after he realizes that you're still alive, he will be back to chasing you and where does that leave me? I'll still be without him!"

Damn, this bitch is smarter than I gave her credit for, I thought to myself. But, she was dumb as a box of rocks if she thought I was going to let her kill me or put me back in that damn box. She was sadly mistaken if she thought I was going down without a fight.

"Fine then, don't call him. But you have to know that I'm not about to go back in that fucking box. I don't deserve this shit. I ain't did shit to you for you to be keeping me here like this." I had to let her know. Fuck that shit! I was done talking. The funny thing about it was that I was inching closer and closer to her the whole time we were talking.

She opened her mouth, preparing to say something to me, but I was not about to listen to anything else she had to say. Before a word could come out of her mouth, I jabbed her right in her throat. She quickly grabbed herself around the neck, gasping for air. Not giving her time to regain her composure, I pounced on her like a bear. I mauled at her like I was trying to tear the skin from her bones.

As I continued fighting her, sending blow after blow to her face, all she could do was scream and kick. She was begging me to stop whooping her ass, but there was no way I was going to let her get out of this. She was going to pay for ever calling herself holding me against my will.

Very quickly, I jumped off her, making my way to the overturned box that once contained my body. I flipped it back over where it was right side up before heading back towards the woman's body.

Scooping the woman up, I threw her inside the box, closing it as quickly as possible, but not without punching her in the face two more times. I frantically looked around the room for something to keep the door on the box closed.

Pausing in my tracks, I stopped to study the box. This bitch had me inside of an old casket, as if she was planning to bury me alive. I could feel my body beginning to warm up as if my blood was boiling from the realization that Tavares had, once again, put me in harm's way.

When I couldn't find anything to hold the box shut, I hauled ass out the room I was in, looking for a way out of what appeared to be a shed. Remembering I didn't have any clothes on, I scavenged through the shed to see what I could find. The more I hunted around, the more the surroundings of the shed became familiar to me. I was still on the land where Tavares and I once shared a home. The shed was so far away from the house, no one even noticed it being out there.

Treading lightly, I made my way outside the front door where I could hear the bushes wrestling in the wind. It was now nightfall and nothing could be heard, but crickets. It would've been nice if I were able to just walk into the house, take a long hot bath, get dressed, and bounce, but I knew that was definitely out of the question. Instead, I stepped back inside the rusty shed, covered in dust and mold, grabbed the shaggy curtain off the window, and wrapped it around my body.

That's when I started my journey away from the land. I knew it was going to be a long night, but staying there was not an option. There was only one person I knew I could turn to for help right now. My only hope was that they would be willing to help me without getting the police involved.

ꯍ 6 ꯍ

Tavares

"Wesley, I could've sworn I told your ass to take care of Lateshia. Why is she back in my business?" I screamed through the phone, agitated at the fact that he was not following orders the way that I told him to.

"Man, I'm done with all of this. I'm not going back to jail for you. She came at me talking about she was pregnant, when I know damn well I can't have any more kids."

"What the hell does that have to do with what I told you to do? I meant what I said when I told you that I had you. Damn, I should have remembered that the only way to get something done the right way was for me to do it myself."

"Yeah, but I'm not trying to hear that man. You already have me too deep in this shit and now, with your wife missing, they're about to do some deep digging into people that you've had any contact with since the separation. I'm not trying to be caught up."

"Wesley, you should know that once you start working with me, you don't stop involvement with me so easily. You're acting like Kat now. There's no easy way out of dealing with me."

"Are you threatening me? That's what I'm taking it as, so you need to clarify yourself nigga," Wesley strongly spat, questioning me like he was out of his mind.

"I'll tell you what, you didn't do what I asked of you. You should've never signed up for what I asked you to do. Take what I said any way you want to, but know that there are consequences to everything that you do." With that, I hung the phone up. There was nothing left to say. He would be handled, but I knew I was going to have to wait until things died down in regards to Kat's case. I knew Officer Coleman meant what she said about seeing me go down, so I knew that I was going to have to be careful with every move that I made.

Sitting in my empty house was taking a toll on me. I tried to carry on with my life the best way that I could, but it was getting more and more difficult, with people always following me around and watching everything that I did.

Picking up my phone, I started going through my contacts to see who I could call over to get my mind off things. None of the women in my phone could be depended on to come over without becoming too attached.

After careful consideration, I called Margareta into my room. She'd been my housekeeper for the last 3 years. She had an exotic look to her that I really adored. She couldn't have been more than 24 years old. I paid her very well to take care of things around the house, especially when I had to go out of town for business.

Margareta was what I considered to be fun-sized. She stood to be about four feet, eleven inches. She appeared to be Brazilian, but was really a combination of Mexican and Puerto Rican descent. She always wore her hair in a messy ponytail displaying her exotic slanted eyes, full pouty lips, and high cheekbones. The make-up of her body was a close resemblance to Nicki Minaj, minus all that ass.

"Margaretaaaaaa!!" I yelled over the banister of the stairs. The minute she heard me calling her, she came running to see what I needed.

"Yes Mr. Tavarez?" She never could quite pronounce my name correctly, but I wasn't complaining. It sounded good coming from her.

"Well, I was just wondering if you've cleaned my room yet. There are a few spots that looked like they need to be tidied up a bit," I stated to her, lying. Shit, I needed a reason to be calling her in the room.

I knew she knew what I wanted, but things with us had to flow naturally. I didn't want her thinking that she had to sleep with me to keep her job or even get the pay that she got, which, by the way, was more than what most of my other workers received.

"Mr. Tavarez, I have cleaned in here alreadies, but I will clean again if you want me to."

"Yes please. Make sure you focus on the bed. The covers aren't quite the way I'd like for them to be."

"Oh, they look fine to me. How would you like them sir?" she innocently asked me.

"Come on now. You know I'm not picky. You know exactly how I like them."

Blushingly, she pulled all the covers off the bed and walked towards me. "Do you mean when they are scattered all over the floor?" That was exactly what I meant.

Her words were as if she were singing in my ear. That's exactly what I was prepared to make her do, sing my name and beg for more of what I was about to give her. By the time I was done with her, even the neighbors who lived down the road would know my name.

"Mr. Tavarez, are you sure we should be doing this with your wife missing? I just don't feel like it's the right thing to be doing. Mrs. Jordan has been good to me. This would seem so wrong."

I could feel my head jerking back looking at her with the *'bitch are you crazy'* look. Then, I tried to get clarity in what she was saying. "So, you're fine with getting down with me as long as she could be found and she was still living in this house? Now, you feel bad about opening your legs to me? That's the dumbest shit I've ever heard."

"What do you mean that is dumb? What if she's dead?"

"What if she is? That's even more reason for you to let me lay this pipe. Just consider it as a way of consoling me. No other explanation needed," I intensely implied, trying to give her some form of confirmation that it would be okay.

"Now, that's the dumbest shit I've ever heard nigga," she snapped at me. The minute she said that, her accent flew out the window. She jumped hood real quick with the whole neck rolling, lip smacking, and finger pointing.

"Damn, chill out hoe! I was just making an observation of something," I calmly stated to her, trying to do my best not to smack her across the room for all the back talking she was doing.

"Hoe? Did you really just call me a hoe? You're the one who's the hoe! You're also a slut, liar, cheater, manipulator, and just all around bastard for not being able to keep your dick in your pants. Yeah, you have a mighty big package, but you have no stamina at all. I have to do all the work to reach my peak when I'm with you. Now, I'm going to finish my work and the minute you try to fire me or withhold my money, I'll go to the police about us and what really happened the night Mrs. Jordan came up missing."

All I could do was stand there. What did she mean by telling them what happened the night Kat came up missing? That was her off day, so she shouldn't have been anywhere near the house that night. Thinking fast, I was in pursuit of her like we were in a high-speed chase. I had to figure out exactly what she knew before she did try to run to the police.

"Margareta, hold up," I stated once I was upon her. I jerked on her arm, turning her to face me. "What do you mean by tell the police what happened the night my wife disappeared? What do you know? And what happened to your accent?"

"I live in the hood and I am also mixed with black, so you should know that I'd have an ounce of ratchet in me. Furthermore, I was here the night your wife came up missing. When things started going left between y'all, I jetted out the door to avoid being a witness to anything further."

She turned to walk away from me, but she made a bad move by walking inside the kitchen. Instead of allowing her to continue going on about what she saw, I grabbed a knife and continuously stabbed away at her body. I must've stabbed her about fifty times before I grew tired of stabbing her.

Her lifeless body laid upon the kitchen floor in a puddle of blood.

The blood started to stain the tile, so I knew I needed to move her body quickly and clean up the mess before someone showed up at the house, especially Officer Coleman's worrisome ass. At midnight, I was going to take her further out on the land and lay her to rest at the abandoned shed I had.

7

L*ateshia*

After everything that went down with Tavares, I had to let my parents know what was going on. Instead of telling them about it on the night of the altercation, I waited until the next day when I could get them alone. Explaining everything to them was going to be hard for me to do, but I knew it had to be done.

They wanted to stay at Kat's house hoping that she would return, but the police had it taped off. They didn't want anyone going in there until they could do further investigation into her missing person's case. With my father's recent altercation with Tavares, there was no way they were going to stay with him. That just meant that they had to stay at my house with me.

Marching into my living room, I felt confident enough to explain things to them. I hated to do it; I just knew they would be hurt by everything I've done just as much as Kat was, but there was no way around telling them.

"Mom? Dad? Can I talk to ya'll now?" I shyly probed, hoping it would cause them to show me some type of pity.

"If you aren't about to tell us the truth, then no, we would not like to hear what you have to say," my father promptly and seriously stated to me. That was a tell-tale sign that he was mad at me and this whole situation.

"Go ahead dear," my mother advised, allowing me to tell her what was on my mind.

"Last night, when Tavares told you about what happened between us…" I paused at the feeling of tears forming inside of my eyes. I really didn't want to shed another tear, but I knew that it would hurt them more than it was going to hurt me to tell them what I had to say.

"Well, go ahead Lat. We don't have all day for this foolishness," my father demanded again. He was about to start pissing me off, rushing me into admitting something I didn't want to admit.

"I did engage in an affair with Tavares, but it was never intentional. We were drinking and it just happened. It was so long ago and only happened once. I've regretted it ever since it happened. Kat was informed about it, which is why she and I have an estranged relationship."

"Stop it Lateshia!" my mother blurted out. She appeared to be angry. I wasn't sure if it was because I'd just told her about what happened between Tavares and me or if it was something else.

"What do you mean stop it? I'm telling you what happened between Tavares and me. You did tell me to tell you what happened."

"You told us what you thought we wanted to hear. We learned a long time ago from Kateshia what you'd done. We know you slept with her husband multiple times and even went as far as trying to be in a relationship with him, but that didn't work out in your favor. How many times are you going to keep lying? When will these charades with you end?"

"What are you talking about? I'm telling you what happened. Kat just told you what she wanted you to hear. Why are you always taking up for her?"

"Hmmm… let's see here; you've done nothing but been a nuisance since you were younger. Do you know how many times I walked in and caught you fucking your own father? Yeah, I knew about all of that, but I never said a word. It kept me from having to be with him sexually. You had to wonder what the real reason was that I treated you and your sister so differently."

The dam broke and liquid flowed down my face. How did she ever find out what happened? That was something I never wanted anyone to know. There I was, resenting my mother for thinking she was treating Kat better than me, just to be doing it, and all along, she really did have a reason to resent me. I'd never been an introverted person. I always found myself to be the life of the party, hanging out and engaging in numerous relationships when I was younger. I was drinking, smoking weed, and popping pills. You name it, I did it.

When I was fourteen, I was sent home early from school. I was suspended for fighting with this thot that accused me of sleeping with her man. Even if I was, there was no real evidence of me doing so. She was just going off hearsay. Needless to say, she got the upper hand of me with the help of two of her girls. That reminds me that I need to hit that trick with my car the next time I see her.

Anyway, I went to my room and popped a few ecstasy pills waiting for the same boy I was jumped over to get out of school and come see me. I was texting him while he was still in class and he canceled on me. I was so furious that I decided to go for a run. I threw on some tights and a sports bra. Lacing up my tennis shoes, I headed towards the front door, bumping into my father on my way out.

He came in the house saying he had a headache and wanted to go lay down. I told him to sit in the living room and I'd bring him some aspirin and seltzer water. Before I went into the kitchen, I ran to my room to grab an ecstasy pill, then went into the kitchen and got the water. I trotted into the living room handing him the pill and water, telling him to drink up.

"Thanks Lat. I really hope this helps this headache," he said to me as he put the pill in his mouth, using the water to chase it down. I stood in front of him watching him the whole time, allowing the ecstasy time to kick in. When I noticed his manhood starting to rise, I maneuvered my way behind him and began to massage his shoulders. His head went a little limp, as it hung down towards his chest waving side to side the more I massaged him.

Moving around in front of him, I started grinding against his rod. I could feel it continuously getting harder. He was letting out soft, sensual moans. The more he did it, the more turned on I became. When he appeared to be very comfortable and in a zone, I pulled his pants down and dropped to my knees. I began to fill my mouth with his manhood inch by inch. It was definitely fulfilling to me and causing my mouth to be filled with more and more saliva. As I was trying to suck the meat off his bones, I was slowly removing my tights. Standing up, I turned and straddled my father to ride him reverse cowgirl style. The rest of that was history.

Let me explain something, I've always had a high sex drive. My father was quite a handsome man. He was an identical match to Common. I knew that I was wrong for seducing him, but I was horny and so was he. We fooled around a few times after that, when we were sure no one was around or would be heading to the house.

We stopped once I started dating Darnell. We both knew that it was wrong and that it was something that we couldn't continue doing. But, I had no idea my mother knew about it or that it was the reason that she really acted differently towards me than she did to Kat.

"Do you not hear me talking to you? Are you ready to explain why you've chosen the role of being the side bitch to every man that comes into your life? Do you realize that since you've reached the age to date, you've never brought a man to the house for us to meet?"

"What does that have to do with anything? There's never been a man worthy enough to meet my parents," I lied through my teeth. Truth was, Wesley was the ideal candidate to meet my parents, but he turned out to be like the devil in a blue dress.

I wanted to talk to my parents about what happened with him and the possibility that I may have AIDS, but they were so concerned with what was going on with Kat and bringing up the fact that my father and I'd fooled around. Now, was really not the time for her to be bringing up things of the past for me.

"You know what, this isn't the time for any of this. We're supposed to be focusing on Kat and what happened to her," I urgently tried to change the topic at hand.

"Yeah, you would be concerned with your sister's well-being when the things you've done have now started to catch up with you. You can feel the scorching heat burning your ass, huh?"

"Mother, I'm not going to disrespect you, so I'm just going to drop the subject. I really needed to talk to ya'll about something that was going on with me, but, yet again, everyone is only seeing my fault. I will not deal with this any longer tonight."

"Lat, if you weren't my daughter and we weren't already in a midst of a situation right now, just know that you could've definitely counted on me. Do you want to know what you could've count on me for?"

"And what would that be mother?"

"You could've counted on me to whoop that ass," she screamed as she stormed out of the room with tears streaming down her face.

My father remained in the room during the entire altercation looking shell-shocked. Not one time did he try to take up for me. He didn't even bother to acknowledge that he was just as guilty as I was in all of this.

With my mother not talking to me, my father playing dumb, my sister missing, and me not knowing what's really going on with my health, I didn't know how things could get any worse for me. I just knew I needed to talk to someone and soon.

8

Darnell

Knock... Knock....

Lying in the bed with the newspaper across my chest, I could feel a lonely tear drop brushing down the side of my face. There was a knock on my door that I was trying to ignore, but the constant knocking let me know that they had no intentions of going away.

Dragging myself out the bed, I moved over to the window, to glimpse out the curtain. To my surprise, Cameron was standing on the opposite side of the door, but how the hell did he find me? Traveling over to the door, I pulled it open, hurriedly yanking Cameron inside the room while being sure to stick my head out, surveying the surroundings. I needed to be sure no one had followed him and if he was setting me up as payback for standing him up the last time we were supposed to be together or for telling him that I didn't want to build anything with him, then he would have to deal with me later.

"How did you find me?" I instantly inquired.

"I had a tracking device put on your car a while back. I could've come to you a long time ago, but I know you didn't want our business out in the open. The press has been slandering you, thanks to that

Tavares guy. Until Kat reappears, things won't be looking good for you. Have you decided what you were going to do?" He inquisitively asked.

"I'm supposed to be meeting my attorney at the police station in a few," I nervously replied, looking over at the clock. I had an hour to get to the police station and hadn't even begun to get dressed.

"Would you like for me to come with you as support? Or I can be there to bail you out if they decide they're going to keep you for her disappearance. Rumor has it that she's dead though."

"Cameron, don't come in here with that negative shit. She isn't dead. Besides, there's no body and no real evidence that I had anything to do with her disappearance, other than her jealous ass husband."

"Yeah, but the story that he provided to the police has floated through the media. Everyone is showing him a lot of pity. The fact that you and Kat both came up missing and you reportedly were upset because she dumped you to go back to her husband puts you at a major disadvantage."

"Oh, come on Cameron, you know me better than most people. Do you seriously think I could kill Kat? I mean, damn, you of all people knew how much I loved her."

"Pfft.... don't remind me of you loving her. I'm still pissed off about how you did me in regards to her. That shit was nowhere near cool."

"Hang on a minute, I need to freshen up, so I can go meet with my attorney. You can at least drive me to the police station, but no, I don't want you sticking around. I can always call you if I need you to pick me up. I just have to clear my name."

"Yeah, whatever you need me to do boo," he cheerfully stated, as he grabbed my ass when I turned to walk away from him.

"It's not that kind of party playa," I shot back at him, letting him know that I wasn't prepared to go there with him again.

I scurried to the bathroom to shower, so I could get ready to go before the police. I knew they already had me pegged as being guilty before they even heard my side of the story. This whole mess with Kat had done nothing but ruin my life. With each passing day, I'd regretted reaching out to her. Even when she found out about the situation with her sister and me, she ran without hearing me out. I should've taken that as a sign to stay as far away from her as I could.

Now, standing in the shower allowing the water to beat over my body, I could feel a hand start to caress my back. I just knew I was envisioning Kat standing in the shower with me, anticipating me entering her from behind.

My manhood was more erect than normal, causing me to begin massaging it. I knew for sure that I was missing Kat and everything about her. I wanted to slide into her tight, wet space that only I could occupy perfectly.

I was so caught up in my thoughts of Kat that I could suddenly feel her mouth tightly grasping the tip of my joystick, allowing me to let out a lenient whimper. I imagined placing my hand behind her head, moving it at a speed that would give me immense pleasure. With a mouth full of saliva, her mouth moved up and down my rod.

Using her hand, she began to massage my sac, increasing the speed in which she was sucking me off. I could feel my eruption coming as she increased her pace of sucking, almost sending me over the edge, only to slow back down, stopping me from erupting like a volcano. Looking down into her catlike eyes, I could tell she was enjoying pleasing me as much as I was enjoying receiving the pleasure.

Not being able to take her teasing anymore, I pulled her to her feet and pinned her against the wall, sliding my massive erect shaft inside her wetness. I could feel her reaching between her legs, extending her hands and continuing to caress my balls while I was drilling her from behind. I was pounding her insides so hard that I almost thought I cracked one of her ribs. Finally, we both wailed out in complete elation as we both reached intense orgasms.

"That was so good boo," I heard a male's voice say as I opened my eyes and realized that it was in fact Cameron in the shower with me and not Kat. I was immediately repulsed at what had just transpired between us again.

I knew that was going to be something I'd have to address in the near future, but right now, I needed to make it to the police station to meet my attorney. Cameron and I both dressed fleetingly, then made our way to his vehicle. Swerving in and out of the rush hour traffic, we made it to the police station with minutes to spare.

"Hello, Mr. Ashford," I communicated to my attorney as I held out my hand in order to shake his.

"Hello, Darnell! Are you ready to get this over with?" he quizzed, looking over the rim of his glasses.

"I'm as ready as I'll ever be. I told you everything that happened and about the things that occurred up until her disappearance. Hopefully, they will hear me out, instead of slapping cuffs on me and throwing me into a cell."

Making our way inside the police station, it appeared that news vans came out of nowhere. Before we could make it inside the door good, reporters were running towards us to question where me about where I'd been and if I knew where Kat was. I wanted to turn around and answer their questions, but my attorney advised me it would be in my best interest if I didn't say anything. At least not until after I'd spoken to the police.

"Hello, we are here to speak with the detective working the Kateshia Jordan case." I heard my attorney state to the receptionist behind the desk.

"Please have a seat and someone will be with you momentarily," she replied.

Instead of having a seat, we stood there patiently waiting for the detective. "Are you sure you've told me everything that I need to know? I'd hate for the media to dig up some dirt that I'm not prepared to deal with," Mr. Ashford warned. He was one of the best in the game. Even if he knew you were guilty, he'd still fight like hell to get you off. *Now, who did that remind you of?* I thought as I chuckled to myself.

"Good afternoon, gentlemen. I'm Detective Woods and I'm assigned to Kateshia Jordan's case. This is my partner, Detective Eisenhower," the detective stated, extending her arm so that we could shake her hand. With the introductions and handshakes out the way, we headed to the back to sit in one of the interrogation rooms.

Detective Woods stated the interview was going to be recorded for accuracy and in the event that I make a confession. I wasn't trying to hear anything about a confession. That was not something they were about to get from me.

"That's fine. I'm just here to clear things up. I'm being considered as a suspect in the disappearance of Kateshia, based off information you received from her husband. True enough, I was in the house the night she came up missing, but I was definitely not the one who saw her last." I laid everything on the line for them, giving them the history between Kat and me from high school up until the last time we were together. My attorney presented them with phone records, hotel receipts, and emails verifying everything I was saying.

Tavares tried to be slick and turn everything around on me, but now the tables were turning. He was about to find out real quick what happened when you mess with someone who dealt with mentally unstable people on a daily basis. To me, he was asking for a fight and I was more than ready to give him one. With my attorney by my side and all the evidence I had, there was no way in hell I'd be going down for anything.

9

C*ameron*

I couldn't have been happier to walk in on Darnell in deep thought over Kat's horse mouth ass. Watching him stroke his manhood instantly turned me on. In my mind, he needed to release some stress and I just so happened to be in the right place at the right time. His long, thick sausage had me craving to taste him. Instantly, I snatched my clothes off, allowing them to land scattered on the floor while I quietly made my way into the shower with Nell. Dropping to my knees, I inserted his rod in my mouth as if I were a slot machine being fed coins. A nigga was thankful Nell was so caught up in the moment that he didn't realize what was happening until it was almost said and done.

As I sat in the car waiting for him to hopefully walk out of the police station, I started to think about a lot of things that had transpired over the past few years within my own personal life. See, Darnell didn't know that the real reason for me separating from my wife was due to her walking in on me drilling another man. That was need to know information, if you asked me. Besides, what would that have to do with us being together?

Yeah, I'm still mad about the way things went down when we were back in Washington and, soon enough, Darnell would pay for abandoning me for Kat, but I had to get him out of this sticky situation he was in. I knew it wasn't going to be easy to do because of the evidence stacked against him. Considering all things, Tavares provided a statement pretty much naming Darnell as a suspect in Kat's disappearance and they both went missing.

What's crazy to me was that Darnell still had his phone on him. If I could find him, I know the police should've been able to find him by now. There was something really suspicious about how everything was playing out if you ask me.

Then, there was still the issue with Afreeca. She was working with me to make things bad between Kat and Darnell, but she was really stuck on making Darnell hers. There was no way I was going to allow that to happen and she should've known that. Everything that we've worked to do to make things bad in his life was for me to be able to step in and pick up the pieces for him. For me, that was the sure way to get him to see that I was in his corner and would be there for him for anything. Since things weren't working out the way that we set them in motion to be, I had to rethink my plan. The only difference was that, this time, they would not involve Afreeca or anyone else.

When I showed up at the hotel room, I didn't know what I was going to say to him. Although I hated he was in the situation he was in, the deeper he got in it, the more it worked out in my favor. I'm sure if Kat wasn't missing and he didn't need anyone to be on his side, he probably wouldn't have opened the door for me. While it is sad for me to say this, I kind of wish that Kat was dead, so that I could divert Darnell's attention back to me. Everything with us was fine until he started talking to Lateshia and found out that things with Kat and Tavares were going down the drain. That somehow set shit in motion for him to try to step up and be her man. He should've left well enough alone.

Either way you look at it to me, I think it's fucked up how he used me to handle his sexual needs but was quick to drop me like a load of trash from yesterday the minute he thought he could get in good with Kat. She wasn't the one there for him when he almost lost his job for getting too personal with a client. But, I'm sure he never told her that secret. She wasn't there when he went through his nasty divorce. Neither was she there when he had the flu, had that stomach virus giving him the bad case of shits, or when he broke his damn leg trying to play basketball. The dummy thought he was Jordan and went up to dunk the ball and landed wrong on his leg. I was there to take care of him when he had no one else and, at the snap of a finger, he forgot about all of that shit. Well, I was not going to let things fly like that. He was going to remember all the shit that I've done for him and he was definitely going to return the favor.

Truth was, I'm tired of having to hide who I am. I couldn't help the fact that I'm in love or that I'm in love with a man. Why should it matter anyways? People always say there's someone out there for everybody and it just so happens that the person that was out there for me was also working with a bat and two balls between his legs. Besides, it's not like we ask other people to watch us have sex, nor do we do that public display of affection shit. I just feel like I should be able to be out in the open about my relationship just like everyone else.

So, what if we aren't in a relationship yet? It was going to take a little convincing, but I'm pretty sure I could get Darnell to see that I'm the one for him. Not Kat, not Lateshia, and damn sure not Afreeca. I'll show him, just wait and see. Right now, I'm going to sit my happy go lucky ass out here patiently in this car and wait for my boo to come out of the police station. At some point, I knew his ass would be ready to ride out in the sunset with me. Don't believe me, just watch!

❧ 10 ❧

Kateshia

After two tedious hours of begrudgingly walking through the woods and back roads, I reached my destination. I don't think I've ever been so happy to make it somewhere in my life. All the stopping to rest, gradual walking, having to watch my step due to being barefoot, and the 30-mile distance was the reason it took as long for me to arrive. It would've been easy for me to try to sneak in my old home and grab my car keys or catch a ride, but if Tavares reported me as being missing, I didn't want to risk anyone recognizing me.

Walking up the long driveway, I found myself having to stop again, due to being out of breath. Something was going to have to give. This easily being out of breath was not sitting well with me. Maneuvering around the house to the backyard, the motion light popped on as soon as it could sense my movement. I stood there frozen in my tracks, praying that I wasn't about to be caught.

After a good two minutes of no additional movement, I proceeded to the back door. Knocking on the door, I could hear someone in the kitchen. Standing on my tiptoes, I tried to look through the window to see if I could see anyone. When I saw nothing, I knocked on the door a little harder. I kept knocking until I could hear someone on the other end belch out, "Who the hell is it and why are you behind my house?"

"It's me! Please open the door."

"Kateshia, is that you?"

"Yes, it's me. Please open the door!" Within seconds of me announcing myself, the door flew open. Michael stood there with a look of shock on his face.

"But, how did you- Where have you-" He muttered off partial questions without giving me time to answer either. When I prepared to open my mouth to speak, Michael grabbed me up in a bear hug and swung me around. He was holding on to me so tight that I felt like I was going to lose consciousness.

When he realized how snug we were, he finally let me loose. "We have to call the police. You've been on the news as a missing person. Where the hell have you been Kat?" he worriedly quizzed, looking my body over to see if I would need medical attention.

"I'm fine, Michael. I don't want to call the police right now. I'm going to get through this without them. Tavares has these cops in his back pocket. He's going to pay for what he did to me before I attempt to get this missing person's mess cleared up. But, please allow me to take a bath and eat before I do anything else."

"Damn Kat, you need to go to the hospital and be checked out. Did he hurt you? Were you raped? Where have you been? Tell me something damn it," Michael scolded loudly, causing me to damn near jump out of my skin.

"Michael, I will explain everything to you. If you'll just allow me to eat and take a hot bath first, then I'll lay everything out on the table. I also need clothes to put on. As you can see, mine somehow managed to be replaced."

"Ok, you sit right here and let me go run you a hot bubble bath. While you're in the tub, I'll run to your favorite Chinese place to get the General Tso's chicken and shrimp fried rice that you like. That way, you can eat once you get out the tub. We can talk while you eat and you can sleep in my guest room."

Michael listed out my exact order from my favorite Chinese restaurant. Under normal circumstances, I would've thought that was cute that he was able to remember things that I enjoy. However, I'd never told Michael my favorite restaurant, let alone what I ordered from there. I should've said something, but I decided to let it go since he was willing to help me. But you better know that I was going to stay on his ass to find out how the hell he knew so much about me without me telling him.

"Yeah, you do that. I just want a bath, some food, and a bed. That's all I want right now. I'm overly tired and I feel so dirty."

"Follow me to the guest room. It has a bathroom in it where you can have privacy. I'll grab a t-shirt and some boxers for you to put on when you get out. I'll also get you a pair of socks; those feet looking a tad bit rough," Michael jokingly stated, causing me to playfully pop him upside the head.

Michael turned to pick me up and carried me to the designated room. Once inside of there, he placed me on the bed and proceeded to the bathroom. I could hear him turning the water on. He was saying something to me, but I couldn't quite make out what it was.

I hopped off the bed, heading towards the bathroom to see what he was saying, but not before observing the room. It was beautifully decorated and had a homey feel. Fully furnished, I could tell that he had hired someone to do the decorating for him.

Finally turning to go inside the bathroom, I bumped right into Michael. "What are you doing?" he probed with a peculiar look on his face. The look in his eyes was one that I'd never seen before. It was bizarre, kind of like he was zoning out.

"Oh, I was headed to see what you were saying. I could hear you talking out here, but I couldn't quite make out what you were saying. Before I came inside the bathroom, I took another glimpse of the room, admiring it."

"Is everything okay with the room? If not, you can go inside of another room; I have more."

"I would imagine you would have more. Why do you have this big old house by yourself anyways?" I pried.

"I'm a big boy and I like big things. Is there anything wrong with that?"

"Nope, nothing wrong with that at all," I quickly returned. "I was actually admiring how nice it was put together. Your decorator did an excellent job. Anyways, what were you talking about when you were in the bathroom?"

"I was actually on the phone ordering the food. That would give me enough time to run your bath, grab your clothes, and make sure the room is straight while they're fixing the food. Since everything appears to be good in here, I'm going to head on to pick the food up. I'll put the clothes on the bed before I go. If you need anything else, just let me know."

"I don't have a way to call you. Remember, I'm missing?" I teasingly retorted to him.

"Well, grab my house phone if you need to call me. I'll grab a prepaid phone for you while I'm out, so you can have a way to make contact with someone if you need to without worrying about the call being traced."

"Thanks for doing all of this for me, Michael. I promise, it will all work out soon, then I'll be out of your hair," I indicated, walking closer to him and kissing him on the cheeks. I could see him blushing a bit. I hope I wasn't giving him the wrong impression because a relationship was definitely not something I was looking for.

"Not a problem boo. I'm going to get the food and your phone. I'll be back shortly. Take as much time as you need and make yourself at home."

When he turned to walk away, I zoomed into the bathroom, threw the curtain I was wrapped in on the floor, and jumped in the tub. I submerged my whole body in the water and received pure ecstasy. A week without a bath was the worst thing that could've happened to me. Going a day without one was detrimental to my health if you ask me. So, I was going to lay there and enjoy that bath as long as I could.

☙ 11 ❧

Michael
Shocked was not the word for what I felt when I opened my door and saw Kat standing there. For the life of me, I couldn't figure out how she got to my house when she was supposed to be missing. The bright side to that was that she did think to come to me in a time of need. That meant that I'd managed to gain her trust.

While she was in the tub, I rushed out the house to grab her something to eat. On my way back to the house, I stopped at the Dollar General store and picked up a Tracfone for her. It'd have to be her source of communication with the outside world until she got through this mess.

When I made it back to the house, she was still in the guest room getting herself together, so I took some plates out of the cabinet and put the food on it. I made a nice little spread on the dining room table with the food, some wine, fruit, and a little brownie for dessert. I was trying to give her something that she'd appreciate and that would be really edible to her since she said she hadn't had anything worthwhile to eat in over a week.

For the life of me, I couldn't wrap my mind on how she'd been able to survive if she wasn't able to eat. I couldn't wait until she came into the dining room to join me for dinner. I really wanted to know the details of what happened to her.

As I was finishing up with setting everything up on the table, Kat came walking into the room. She looked very radiant. I couldn't believe all the things Tavares put her through and was still willing to put her through, only so he could be in control of her.

"I feel so much better. Thanks again for letting me crash here."

"Kat, what's the plan? I want to help you, but I need to know what's going on. You know I'll always have your back, but I don't want to be caught in the middle of anything that could land me behind bars."

"Michael, I'd never do anything that would get you arrested. I plan on going to the police over the next few days, but I need to figure a few things out. Tavares is going to pay for the part he's played in this. What I don't get it is why I ended up in that shed," Kat continued to talk, as she made her way over to the table to take a seat where her plate was sitting.

"Is it okay for us to talk about things right now? I don't want to pry, but we have to figure out what happened and what we're going to do to get you out of this mess." I suggested we get some paper and start writing down the things she could remember about what happened from the time she came up missing until the time she showed up at my house. Hopefully, she could come up with some answers to questions that she had herself.

"That's fine. We can write things down, but give me a minute because I'm about to murder this plate," she said jestingly. She was joking when she said it, but she was killing that food. You would've thought she was an inmate in prison trying to glut down her food before another inmate came over there trying to Debo her plate.

"Slow down before you choke killa! You're really smashing that food."

"Told you I haven't eaten in over a week. I could've died. No one will ever be able to really imagine the things I've gone through. The only way I was able to survive without really dehydrating is by drinking my piss. I know it sounds gross, but I had to do what I needed to do in order to survive." I could see her look up at my face to see if I was going to frown up at what she said to me. I did my best to keep a straight face, no matter how nasty that shit sounded to me.

"Tell me what happened. Something had to be going on for you to end up where you were. And you said it was someone that you'd run into before; maybe she said or did something that could help you identify who she was and what was her reasoning behind taking you."

"The last thing I can really remember was going back home to complete six months of being with Tavares. Remember, he told me that if I could get through six months of trying to make things work with him, then he would sign the divorce papers if things don't work out?" When she looked over at me looking for a response, I simply nodded my head at her.

"Well, I started back talking to Darnell. We would hook up in different hotels to be together until I came up with the plan to have sex in the bed that Tavares and I once shared. Tavares came home and caught us, which was what I wanted to happen. What I wasn't expecting to happen is what came after he caught us," she cringed as she informed me of what happed. Sadness took over me as I observed her putting her head down. I could see the tears starting to roll down her face as she silenced herself from talking any further.

"I'm sorry that this is bothering you and you've had to go through that catastrophe, but I really need you to continue to talk. We have to figure out what's the best way to approach this. You're going to have to let the police know that you're alive and well."

"I'm going to let them know, but it'll be a few days before I do that. I plan on putting an end to everything that's been going on with me. All that mess involving Tavares will be no more."

"What do you mean by that? Are you planning to do something crazy?" I curiously inquired. It sounded to me as though she was planning to kill or cause harm to someone. Both are things that could get her put in jail and I didn't want to see that happen to her.

"Look, for over a year, Tavares has put me through hell. I'm not standing for it anymore. I have to get this handled and get my life back on track before I lose everything that I've worked so hard for. Let's just finish eating and we can talk about how things went down a little later."

I looked at Kat and she appeared to be overwhelmed and exhausted. Nobody deserved that, but she wouldn't have to fret. I was going to do everything in my power to make sure she was good.

12

*L*ateshia
     My mother was no longer talking to me, which was very awkward considering they were staying in my house. If I was really a bitch, I would've made them go stay with Tavares or even a hotel. I would've preferred they took their asses back home to Mississippi, but of course, I knew that wasn't going to happen as long as Kat was missing.

My father really hadn't said anything to me either. I needed to find my sister urgently. I was about to explode with everything going on with me.

I was recently diagnosed with schizophrenia. Nobody knew that but me. It was eating me up inside, which had me feeling as though I was going to have a nervous breakdown. And, in case you didn't know, schizophrenia is a mental disorder where someone becomes withdrawn from reality. That explains why I often perceived what happened between Darnell and me as rape. He wasn't even my first. I wasn't going to let him know that though. What kind of idiot would I look like telling people that I was having sex at a young age or that my father was one of my preferred sexual partners?

"Lat, I need to speak with you," a familiar voice stated, startling me from my thoughts.

I was sitting on the edge of my bed gearing up to finally go see Dr. Hines, who had been blowing my phone up relentlessly.

Turning to look at my father's tear-stained face, I couldn't believe the nerve of him to want to talk now.

"What do you want?" I rudely quizzed. "You didn't have much to say when your wife was addressing me about something you and I both engaged in. Nor did you have anything to say anytime after things were put out in the open. So, tell me what you could possibly have to say to me right now."

I was angrier than I thought at the fact that he never stepped up when my mother was chastising me about something I didn't do alone.

"Honey, I know you're upset with me. I would feel the same way if I was in your shoes, but I honestly didn't know what to say, and I didn't want to make matters worse. Do you realize that, if your mother wanted to be vindictive that she could have me arrested for molesting you? See, you're only thinking about yourself; I, on the other hand, was looking at the bigger picture."

"Dad, there's no bigger picture to any of this. We screwed each other's brains out and we both enjoyed it. Of course, we stopped because we both grew tired of the constant sneaking around and looking over our shoulders, praying not to get caught. Just thinking about it now, who's to say we wouldn't have still been sleeping together if we weren't so paranoid about other people finding out."

I knew my father was right about us ending it being the right thing to do. However, that still doesn't make up for the fact that he acted like a coward when my mother brought the situation to the light. Now, he wanted to come to me like everything should be okay with us. He better guess again.

"I'm not even mad at you. You aren't the first person I've encountered that has tried to save their own ass when it came down to picking between sticking up for me or covering their own ass. So, I completely understand. I have a lot of things going on with me and I don't have anyone to talk to. Now, if you'll excuse me, I need to get to a doctor's appointment," I stated, brushing past him while attempting to exit the kitchen.

Grabbing my arm, he turned me towards him with a look of worry on his face. "Why are you going to the doctor? What's wrong with you?"

"Does it even matter? Y'all have been so consumed with the stuff going on with Kat that neither of you have thought to ask me how I was doing. I don't even know why I thought this would be different. She was and always will be the shining star in both of your lives. Damn Lateshia, right?!?"

"Now, you know that's not true. You're the one who left the house without looking back. You're the one who got special attention from me, especially with us sleeping together. If you can't see that, then something really is wrong with you," he patronizingly retorted.

He was starting to get on my nerves. I would never purposely disrespect my parents, but he was begging for me to go HAM on him.

"Well, if you must know, I met this guy a few months ago, and I thought things between us were good. That was until I started to feel sick. So, I went to the doctor and was told that I was pregnant. However, while I was at the doctor's office, I was told that I needed to be tested for STDs."

"So, what's the problem? They test women for all kinds of things when they're pregnant to make sure they're able to appropriately monitor the safety of the mother and child."

"I'm not sure. I ain't ever been pregnant before."

"I think you should be excited about having a baby. This could be the very thing you need to turn your life around."

"What's wrong with my life?" I quizzed, becoming annoyed at the fact that he was apparently judging me. He was out of his mind if he thought I was going to stand there and allow him to act like he was holier than thou. He had the game messed all the way up.

"No, you keep talking about things with you and Tavares was a mistake. Then, there was the situation between you and me. There has to be a balance somewhere and you really could use something positive in your life."

"You would be right if this was something positive for me. Ever since I found out, things in my life seemed to have taken a turn for the worse."

"What do you mean Lateshia? You say people never show concern for you, but don't you think it could be that you don't want to let people in on what's going on with you?"

I knew he was right. I've lost trust for most people, so there's no reason for me to try to tell them what was going on with me. There was no way I was going to give them anything to use against me later. However, since my father was now finally taking the time to listen to me, I was going to unload on him as much as I could about my situation. I was tired of going through this alone and allowing things to build up would only cause me to pop like a cork later.

"Dad, I've caused so much turmoil in the lives of others that things are finally starting to turn around and bite me in the ass. You'd never understand the things I've done or have been through since I left home."

"Well, tell me what it is. And be honest, Lateshia. Nobody can help you if you keep lying or keeping things to yourself. Remember to tell the truth and shame the devil. He expects you to fail at doing right, but we raised you better than that. It's time to take those thongs off if you can't wear them appropriately and put your big girl panties on."

For some reason, hearing him talk about me in thongs really did sound weird to me. I wonder why the thought of my father being inside of me used to seem so natural in the past, but even now, I realize how damn nasty that really was.

"I may have AIDS!" I subconsciously blurted out.

"I know you aren't trying to say I gave it to you," he fumed.

"No idiot. I was dating this guy a few months back and he never told me that he was positive for anything. We ended up having sex a couple of times and when I told me about being pregnant, he started telling me all kinds of things that he was keeping from me. That includes him having a vasectomy and him having AIDS." Geez, there went the stream of water occupying my face, ruining my makeup.

Staggering to take a seat, my father grabbed his chest like he was Fred Sanford. I guess it was too much for him to handle. I hated to tell him the way that I did, but I had no choice.

"Wow, Lateshia, I'm sorry you've had to go through that alone. When are you going to find out what your results are?" he inquired.

"Well, the doctor's office has been blowing up my phone for me to come back in for my results, which is actually where I'm heading now. The fact that they've called me so much has only confirmed that I tested positive. I was so scared of hearing them say it to me, so I've been ignoring their calls. I'm taking it upon myself to go now in order to get this over with."

"Well, let me grab my coat and I'll go with you. I can't imagine how you feel having to go through this alone. I'll be here for you as much as I can. I'm sorry that we failed you as parents."

"Thanks dad! You're here now and that's all that matters," I responded, walking over to him and wrapping him in my arms.

Knock.... Knock... Knock...

I could hear the sound of echoes from someone seemingly beating on my front door. My father and I both looked up at each other as we shrugged our shoulders, implying we didn't know who could be at the door. Jogging towards it, for some strange reason, my heart rate began to speed up. Opening the door, my mouth dropped as I looked up to find a woman with a Health Department badge on standing in my doorway.

❧ 13 ❧

Kateshia
      I've been staying with Michael for a few days now and things have started to become a little strange for me. The way he looked at me had me thinking that he needed to be in a mental hospital. It's like he was staring at a piece of steak, causing him to instantly start salivating. At first, I thought it was cute, but then it started to freak me out.

To top that off, one day I walked in on him having a conversation with someone that he apparently needed to whisper to talk. Of all people, I wondered what he had to hide from me. I thought we were better than that. I constantly prayed that he wasn't telling anyone my whereabouts. Nobody could know that I was alive or where I was until I had things sorted out with how I was going to handle Tavares.

Although I had been laying low, I'd been making plans on how I wanted to handle Tavares. The first thing was to mess up his drug connection with some ugly platypus faced dude named Rock. That was a part of his life that Tavares didn't think I was aware of. He assumed I thought he got all his money honestly, but he must've forgotten how smart I really was.

See, from the time Michael left to go to my office to handle things there for me, I hopped in his Nissan Maxima with the tinted windows, so I could get around town good. Not even Michael knew that I'd been leaving the house and if he did, he sure as hell hadn't let on to me that he knew.

Michael gave me a prepaid card that I could use to order clothes or whatever else I would need while I was with him. I thought that was very generous of him. That was something that he didn't have to do. But since he did, I made it a point to use it to my advantage.

After my first night of staying at his house, that was when he came in with the prepaid card. When he handed it to me, I looked at him like he was crazy. He chuckled at me, then told me what it was for. I wrapped my arms around him to give him a kiss on the cheek again. Seemingly, he wasn't pleased with my gesture of gratitude, so he turned my hug into this big bear hug and planted a kiss right on my lips.

As I looked in his face with shock, I could see that he had his eyes closed. To me, that meant he was kissing me with passion, but there was no reason for him to. There was no passion between us like that. Something seemed off about him, causing any chemistry I thought we had to vanish.

That night when he went to sleep, I did a little online shopping to purchase clothing items for myself, but I also purchased some spyware equipment. I elected for it to be overnighted to me so that I could get to work collecting all the evidence I'd need against Tavares to put him away for good.

Of the many things I bought, cameras, microphones, and a cell phone jammer were on the list. I also purchased some trackers that I could put under the cars, so I could keep up with his locations. I thought it would be hard for me to place the items where I needed around the house, but I decided I would do them little by little so that I'd be able to get in and out undetected.

When the spy equipment arrived, I called Tavares' office to see if he was in. When he picked up the phone, I immediately hung it up. Hearing his voice was all the confirmation that I needed that he was not at home. Collecting all of my equipment, I darted to the car and made my way to my old residence.

Manny was outside on the tractor when I pulled onto the property.

It didn't make sense for him to be out there cutting the grass when the weather was about to get seriously bad. However, I knew that there was no telling Tavares that. He would still have him out there trying to manicure the lawn if it were pouring down raining.

Leaning back in the seat, I sailed past him near the shed that I was once held captive in. Before traveling towards the house, I snatched my bat off the backseat of the car and marched inside the shed. I needed to see if the woman who was holding me hostage was still inside of there. Once I searched through the whole shed, I was able to see that it was vacant. Some kind of way, she'd gotten out of there. This only made me push to work faster, so I could be in and out. I had to get away from that property as soon as I could.

Carefully walking towards the house, I continued to study my surroundings for anything suspicious or that could get me caught. That meant avoiding the workers inside the house too. Arriving at the house, I trotted around to the back. The kitchen door remained open during the day time; that was the door the workers used mostly. Once inside the house, I quickly maneuvered through it, placing the cameras in the bedroom, living room, the basement, and Tavares' office. I chose those specific locations due to those being the places that Tavares favored within the home.

I also placed a phone jammer on each level of the home so that when the time was right and I was prepared to make my appearance to Tavares, I would be able to shut down his outlet to the outside and handle the business I needed to when it came to handling him. When I was done with him, Jesus would be the only person he would need to call on.

Needing to get into the garage, I could hear someone in the kitchen. It sounded like the housekeepers talking about how one of them quit because Tavares kept coming on to them. I wanted to look inside the kitchen to see who they could've possibly been talking about. However, I couldn't look because I was afraid Tavares or someone else would spot me.

"I feel so bad for Mrs. Jordan and her family. She was the best thing that ever happened to us." I could hear one of the housekeeper's state.

"You're right about that. I wish she would've left him years ago and we wouldn't be out there looking for her now," someone responded to her.

They unrelentingly talked about the situation with me missing. I wanted to grab them to hug them so they would know I was okay, but I knew I couldn't. All of this missed time with the ones I loved was starting to get to me. I was going to have to come out of hiding very soon. I just didn't know how much longer I'd be able to do it. That just made my mind ponder on what I would tell the police when I reappeared. It definitely wouldn't involve me trying to take Tavares down. I had to make it look like he was being careless.

Finally, being able to get inside the garage, I managed to put a tracking device on all of his cars, except for the one that he drove all the time. I even decided to put one on my car that was still sitting there, in case he decided to get out of dodge with it.

Making my way back inside the house, the garage door gradually began to rise. That just meant that Tavares was returning back home. Very abruptly, I slid under one of the cars parked in the garage, so he wouldn't see me. My heart was beating so rapidly, I felt as though it was going to leap out of my chest. I knew I wanted to show my face to Tavares, but now definitely wasn't the time to be doing so.

"Aye, I want out of this shit now. With Kat missing, I have 5-0 watching my every move. I can't afford to be caught up in no mess," I heard Tavares bluntly say to whomever he was on the phone with.

"Nigga, take some of that bass out your voice. You acting like a lil bitch because you couldn't control your yapping ass wife and now she's gone. If I know you, you probably killed her and chopped her into little pieces so nobody could find her," was the response the unfamiliar voice on the phone sharply stated.

"Naw, you take the bass out your voice. I'm not one of your lil flunkies and if I was, I still wouldn't allow yo ass to talk to me crazy. Better get your shit together and quit trying me. We need to meet somewhere, so I can give you your money and remaining product. This stops today," Tavares indicated, putting his feet down to let them know what he wasn't going to tolerate. I didn't even see the point of him stomping his feet; it wasn't like the person could see or hear him doing it.

"Ha-Ha-Ha," the person laughed at Tavares as if he really did or said something funny. *"Pardon me for laughing at the shit you spitting to me. What makes you think I'm going to allow you to walk away so easily?"* he solemnly asked Tavares.

"Going to allow me? Nigga, I ain't yo bitch. You don't tell me what I will and won't do. You shole as hell don't feed, fuck, or finance me, which is something you apparently haven't realized yet."

"When and where do you want to meet? You want this to end, so I'll oblige you. But, you better know that when dealing with me, everything comes with a price," the voice gruesomely spoke.

I almost wanted to feel sorry for Tavares for what he had gotten himself into. Then again, how the hell could I feel sorry for someone who didn't feel sorry for all the lying, cheating, abusing, using, you name it, he has done it, to someone; mainly me?

When he was finally in the house, I stayed under the car a few more minutes before coming from under it. I eased the door open to see Tavares walking up the stairs. I closed the door back, trying to give him enough time to make it completely up to the room, so I could get out of the house undetected.

Ten more minutes passed and I dashed out the door like a dog was hot on my ass. I ran out the house without closing the door behind me. I could only hope nobody saw me running from there and follow me to my destination. When I got to the shed, I got inside the car and shot out of there without looking back, making it back to Michael's house in no time.

When I arrived, Michael was in the living room talking on the phone to someone. He called himself whispering, but I could've sworn I heard him say something like "let her get away" and "I could kill you." Those words threw more red flags at me as I pondered over whether I should say something to him or just turn and make an exit out the door.

My phone started ringing abruptly, causing my bones to damn near jump out of my skin. *Who the hell could be calling me when I knew the only person who knew this number was Michael?* I thought to myself.

"I see you finally made it back. Where've you been Kat?" Michael asked me, almost making me piss myself.

"Well, see what had happened was umm..." I couldn't think of anything to say to him that wouldn't keep me from having to tell him where I really was or what I was doing.

"See umm what? Where were you Kat? I thought I told you not to leave the house for any reason."

"No, you never told me not to leave the house. Furthermore, I appreciate you helping me and allowing me to stay here, but if you think you're going to control me in the process, you're sadly mistaken."

He had some nerves thinking he was my father or my damn man. He wasn't shit but a friend and if he didn't learn how to talk to me, then he better learn quickly that I will cut his ass loose and not look back. He had me all the way fucked up if he thought he was going to control my every move. We were in an intense stare down to see which one of us would come out on top. I bet like hell it was going to be me.

❧ 14 ❧

Michael

I know that Kateshia was out of her mind staring at me like she was ready to go toe-to-toe with me. She thinks she's something because she's building herself up to catch Tavares when he least expected it, but she had the game fucked up if she thought she was going to be able to come at me with that same ammo.

Staring into her eyes, I wanted to bend her over the kitchen counter and drill the hell out of her honey pot, but I decided to let her make it. She was sexy as hell in her stare down with me. I'm sure she thought I was engaging in an argument with her, but I was really just using this time to gaze into her eyes. She just didn't understand what she did to me.

"Look Kat, I was just worried about you. You left here and didn't let me know where you were going. You know that being out is not safe for you, with you being all in the media and Tavares looking for you. When he finds you, he's going to try to kill you in order to keep his story going."

"I can understand your concern and I appreciate it, but I can take care of myself. I've been through too much shit to get caught without getting things handled the way I want to see them handled," she barked at me.

I wanted to shake the hell out of her for being so stupid and not listening to what I was saying to her. It made sense what she was saying. I could see how much strength she had gained since going through all of this turmoil with Tavares, but she needed to let me help her.

"What are you planning on doing Kat?" I inquired. I was definitely interested in finding out how she was planning on getting Tavares back for all the mess he'd put her through.

"Michael, I don't want to get you involved in any of this. Just give me a few more days and all of this will be handled."

"Kateshia, stop being idiotic; you need help. This isn't something for you to have to take on by yourself. And in case you haven't realized this yet, I'm already involved. The minute I opened my door to allow you to come in, I was involved."

"That is true, but I'm not trying to put you in this any deeper than you already are. They could think that you helped me fake my disappearance for some strange reason and there could be some jail time behind this."

That was something that I hadn't thought about. *Or what if they found her here and they thought I was holding her hostage? Who's to say that she wouldn't turn on me and say that I was in fact her kidnapper?* Thoughts were flying out of the woodworks of what could happen if I was found to be connected to this in any way.

"This is becoming too chaotic for me. We need to go to the police with what information you have. Darnell was on the news earlier today. You would've known that if you were keeping up with the news," I begrudgingly stated.

After rolling her eyes and stomping her feet, she looked at me and asked, "What was he on the news for?"

"If you must know, he turned himself in; if that's what you're supposed to call it."

"What do you mean turned himself in? He didn't do anything to turn himself in for."

"According to Tavares, it was Darnell who came inside the home attacking both of y'all, only to knock Tavares out and disappear with you. He claimed he was upset about you breaking up with him, so he came in the house with the intent to kill y'all."

"Are you fucking kidding me? Seriously, Tavares didn't tell no bull-shit ass lie like that and hopefully nobody believed it," she stated, then paused with a curious look on her face.

"What are you thinking about?"

"When I got free, I could've easily left the house and went to safety, but I stayed around because I didn't want to leave Darnell in harm's way. When I went back for him, he was gone. Where the hell was he all this time?" she inquired seriously, thinking I would be able to answer that question.

"When he was questioned by the media, he said that he went to a hotel hoping you would call. He claims he's been calling your phone but has been unsuccessful in reaching you."

"So, if he went to the police about everything and they have his side of the story, then why in the world is Tavares still being able to walk around freely?'

"Basically, because it's Tavares' word against Darnell's; then, the fact they don't have a body plays a major factor in all of this as well."

"This just means I need to speed my plan up and get to the bottom of this. All of this has Tavares involved for sure, but I feel like I'm missing something. There's a piece of the puzzle missing somewhere and I'm going to find out what it is."

"Kateshia, just let it go. You need to stop trying to play detective before you end up finding out something you don't want to know. Or worse, you end up being killed," I stated, urging her to quit trying to bring things up that could lead to all of this ending badly.

"It's easy for the people who have the least involvement in all of this to tell me to let it go and just go to the police. But you haven't walked in my shoes, nor have you had to endure all of the bullshit that I've had to for years. This isn't over until I say it's over."

Frustrated with the shit she was spitting at me, I couldn't deal with her anymore. I went from wanting to bend her over the counter and pounding her brains out to wanting to choke the life out of her very quickly. She was starting to get the best of me and I just couldn't allow that to happen. True enough, I wanted her to be mine, but at the shit I'm having to go through, if she doesn't stop all that private investigating shit, she's going to have me sitting in jail right next to Tavares and there is just no way I can allow for that to happen.

❧ 15 ❧

T avares

Today was the day that I was going to cut all ties with my connect Rock. I've had so much heat on my ass since Kat had been gone, so this was the best move for me. He was mad when I told him that I wanted out of the business and, of course, made several threats to me trying to keep me involved in the game, but none of that mattered to me.

It was storming outside. I didn't want to be out in the weather, but this had to end tonight. It needed to end tonight.

Walking through the house, the lights started blinking on and off. That was a new thing to me. I couldn't remember the last time the lights went out in this house, no matter how bad the weather had gotten.

"Tavares," I could hear my name being called in a spooky whisper.

Becoming paranoid, I kept turning around in circles like a dog chasing his tail, trying to see where the whispers were coming from. I knew there was no one else in the house with me. I'd sent the workers home when I realized that the weather was going to be bad. Don't think I was being considerate to them. I just didn't want anything happening that would cause them to be stuck in the house with me. Damn that!

"Tavaresssss!" There was the same noise again. I knew I wasn't going crazy. The voice was too close for comfort.

"Who's there?" I fearfully questioned. If someone answered me, I was out this joint. They could have the house and the furniture that came with it.

Standing in the dark room, I tried to survey my surroundings as lightning bolts continuously shot out of the sky. I tried my best, using each bolt as light to guide my steps. Thinking quickly, I tried to recall where Kat kept the candles in the house. It was times like this that I really missed having her around.

Frustration was not the word to describe how I was feeling. Suddenly, the lights in the house started to flicker on and off again. My eyes must've been playing tricks on me because I could've sworn that in between the lights going off and on, I could see Kat standing at the light switch with a look of hatred in her eyes. Closing my eyes, I rubbed my hands across them before opening them back up. I had to make sure my vision was clear. I couldn't have been seeing her.

Sure as shit, when I opened my eyes, I could still picture Kat controlling the lights in the house. Each time the lights flickered, I inched closer to the switch, which was close to the door. My intent was to get as close as possible without the figure realizing I was moving so that I could grab ahold of them.

"Kat, I know that's you. Why are you doing this? Where have you been?" I quizzed, hoping it would throw her off her game, making her inadvertently answer me. But there was nothing, but silence. The figure continued to stand there, not moving or making a sound.

"Come on Kat, what do you call yourself doing? You think you're going to get away with having people think I killed you?" I asked again, wondering if she was ever going to open her mouth. The more I inched closer to the figure, the more I believed it was Kat.

Finally, getting to the door, the lights went out one last time. I jumped at the doorway and caught nothing, but air. There was no way in hell I was staying in that house another minute. I sure as hell was not about to be running up no damn stairs either. I grabbed my car keys and scattered out the front door.

Listening to my satellite radio, I headed towards the warehouse I was supposed to be meeting Rock at. I hopped on the highway and cruised to my destination. This night couldn't end fast enough for me. I tell you one damn thing; I'll be damned if I go back to that house tonight.

Turning down the street the warehouse was on, I kept passing dark cars with tinted windows along the side of the road. Actually, there were only two cars, but that was more than enough cars than what I was used to seeing. My heart began to race as I got closer to the warehouse.

Looking up to my rearview mirror, it appeared that one of the cars was creeping up behind me. *Was Rock setting me up?* I wondered to myself as I tried to keep a steady pace and decide on what I needed to do. Instead of continuing towards the warehouse, I wheeled my car to the side of the street.

Reaching into my back pocket, I pulled my cell phone out to dial Rock's number. When I didn't get an answer, my suspicions further plagued my mind. Knowing something wasn't right, I made a U-turn in the middle of the street and headed back down the road. I decided I'd text Rock and let him know what was going on.

Me: Aye, something ain't right about tonight. We're going to have to do this another time.

Rock: What you mean do this another time? Either it's tonight or no other time.

Me: Bruh, I'm telling you that the police are camped out by the warehouse. The block is definitely hot. And why the hell are you texting me when you could've just answered the phone when I called?

Rock: Got a bitch eating my dick right now. You took too long to show up.

That was the sign that let me know shit was going awry. If I knew one thing about Rock, it was that his ass was not about to respond when he was with a woman. Now, the million-dollar question was: If Rock wasn't texting me, who the hell was?!?

✣ 16 ✣

Lateshia

The day I opened the door to find the worker from the Health Department at my house, I could've fainted. I didn't know what to do because I just knew she was going to tell me some shit that was going to rock my world.

"Are you Lateshia?" she politely asked me, while extending her hand for me to shake it.

"Yeah, that's me," I returned without shaking her hand. Instead, I turned and walked away, leading the way towards the kitchen. By the time she made it there, I was already sitting down with my father, prepared for what she was going to tell me.

"Hello, I'm Mrs. Scott and I'm a caseworker with the New York State Department of Health. I need to speak with you privately, if you don't mind."

"Of course, she minds. Besides, I'm her father so anything you have to say to her, you can definitely say in front of me," my father protectively stated.

"I agree Mrs. Scott. My father pretty much knows that I've been tested for AIDS, so if you're coming to tell me that I have it, then I'm prepared to hear what you have to say in the presence of my father," I informed her, so that she'd know it was okay to tell me what she needed to say with my father there. Plus, I

really needed him there to be a support system for me. That could explain why I chose to hold his hand the whole time she was talking to me.

"Well, all I can do is respect your wishes. However, before I continue, I do need you to sign this waiver indicating that I've told you that this was a private matter, but you wished to continue with your father present. I also need both of you to sign this form stating that what we discuss will be confidential." With that being said, she began handing us forms to complete.

"Why do I have to complete this form about him being here when you never told me whatever it is you came to say?" I worriedly probed.

"It's actually a part of our policy and if I may be frank with you, it goes along with the "C.Y.A" rule," she oddly specified. It was only odd to me due to her coming in being very professional, then her jumping a little ratchet to tell me she was covering her ass. However, that was understandable and I can't say that I blamed her.

"Well, I do appreciate your honesty, but can we move on with this?"

"Oh yes. If you'd just go ahead and sign the forms, then I shall get this show on the road," she cheerfully spat.

I didn't know what she could be so damn cheerful about when she was about to ruin my life. I talked a lot of shit, but I never thought my life would end with me dying from a disease. Hell, I'd take dying in a freak accident for 'one thousand Alex, I thought to myself as I mocked the people on Jeopardy.

After we signed the forms, I pushed them back across the table to Mrs. Scott. I know I tried to rush her through this process, but I was really about to freak out. I just knew I was about to have a panic attack and pass out. My father must've sensed that I was starting to panic because he reached over and pulled me closer to him.

I thought the men I messed around with were handsome, smart, charismatic, social, and professional. I just knew I was being careful with all the men who supported my living habits or, should I say, that sponsored me. Who would have thought that men who came from backgrounds as the men who I messed with could have any kind of package swinging between their legs other than the meat that was meant to be there? I mean, damn, I didn't ask for them to deliver anything to me, but a good orgasm. They could keep the salmonella to their damn selves.

"Lateshia, I came here because Dr. Hines informed me that she provided you *with some tests while you were in her office. They've tried to contact you on several occasions, but have been unsuccessful in their attempt-"*

Cutting her off, I tried to come up with a reason for being so careless on following up with the doctor's office. "With all due respect,t Mrs. Scott, who wants to have someone tell them that they have AIDS or something much worse?"

"Can I ask you a question Lateshia?"

"Shoot!"

"You keep bringing up AIDS. Is there a reason for this? Have you been in contact with someone who may have it or have you slept with a man that slept with another man?" she nosily solicited.

"Well, I went to the doctor because I thought I was pregnant. Of course, they came back in and said that I was pregnant and gave me prenatal vitamins and iron pills to take. But while I was there, I also ended up being tested for STDs."

"Okay, they test women for that when they come in for their annuals and when they're pregnant. That's nothing to be concerned with and that is definitely nothing unusual."

"So, are you telling me that I don't have AIDS?" I questioned, finding myself becoming jovial at the possibility that I may have misread things. I didn't even bother to tell her what happened between Wesley and me. I was hoping he was just saying that out of anger. Maybe if I didn't claim it, then she'd tell me that it was a false alarm.

"What I'm saying is that you went to the doctor and she provided you with some tests. There was an issue at the lab where your information was mixed with someone else's when the lab tech knocked the test tubes over. The fact that the tubes weren't labeled has caused a frenzy in the clinic and therefore, they need everyone to be retested. The fact remains that someone did test positive for AIDS and before they tell someone they think it may be, they are retesting everyone."

"So, you're telling me that there is a chance that I don't have AIDS?"

"That is exactly what I'm telling you, but we won't know for sure until you take the tests again."

"Well, when will I need to go back for the test and how long will it take for them to let me know something?"

"I'd like for you to go in as soon as possible. You don't have to make an appointment. Dr. Hine's office is waiting for you to appear. They will call you to

the back to take blood samples, scrape in your vaginal area, and take a urine sample. Once this is done, they can send it off to the lab, which will take 3-5 days to return because they will put a rush on it."

"So, I wouldn't have to wait in the waiting area for any of this to happen?" I'm known for being impatient and having to go in the waiting area for them to have to redo something they should've done right the first time was not up my alley. I seriously hated having to wait on anything.

"No, you wouldn't have to wait. Unless they were already tied up having to do labs, which I highly doubt. I mean, it's a clinic and not a hospital, so they shouldn't be on overload when it comes to the number of patients they see in that clinic."

"Okay good, since I was already on my way there, I'll just go ahead and go." I decided to go ahead on my journey there to get this over with.

To be honest with you, these past few days have been taking a toll on me. I've been trying my best to patiently wait for the test results to come back in, but I haven't heard anything. It's crazy how you never know how quickly things can go bad for you. Maybe it was time for me to leave the state of New York and completely start over. Besides, what harm could a little fresh start do?

17

arnell

After going to the police station to let them in on what went down with Tavares, Kat, and me, I felt a sense of relief when they didn't arrest me. Things just didn't add up to me on how Kat was beating Tavares' ass one minute and the next minute, she was gone. That was just too much for me.

I tried texting and calling her phone on several other occasions today, but still there was nothing. The only difference this time was that someone kept sending the phone to voicemail. I'm not a fool. I know that if your phone doesn't have a voicemail, you can't leave a message. If you call and the phone rings for a long period of time, then it went to voicemail on its own. If the phone went straight to voicemail, then the phone is off; but, if you call and it rings maybe two times, then someone sent you to voicemail.

Shaking the hand of my attorney, I walked out of the police station towards Cameron waiting in the car for me. I had to hand it to him; he was determined to get me where he wanted me. That wasn't going to happen because Kat was the person that I wanted, despite all the things I'd gone through to be with her.

"Where to boo?" Cameron asked, as I slid into the passenger seat. I was glad he was posted up where he was because I was able to avoid the news.

"Would you stop with all that boo shit? And what the hell do you call what you did earlier Cameron?"

"What are you talking about boo? I meant to say Nell," he innocently responded.

"I'm talking about you imposing on my shower then sucking me off, knowing I thought you were Kat. You need to chill out with that shit."

"Why do you keep doing this? You want me just as bad as I want you. It's very evident on how you realize it's me and you increase your dick game from zero to one hundred when you try to blow my back out."

"Nigga, quit flossing. You know damn well it's not like that. I have to imagine you're Kat to even get in the mood to bust one. Don't do that shit again Cameron. I'm telling you, I'm done with that shit and if you can't respect that, then you need to walk away from me."

"No. I'm not walking away from you or us. I know we can get through this man. Stop denying your feelings for me."

"That's just it. I have no feelings for you. I was going in because you gave me something to take my mind off Kat. If I was really feeling you, do you think I would've just dropped you so easily when she was back in my life?"

Once I said that to him, he sat there in shock. I guess he never thought about how fast I was to leave him and head back to work things out with her. To me, he was like a toy. I pulled him off the shelf when I wanted to have fun, but then I put his ass right back on the shelf when I was done playing.

"My point exactly," was the response I gave him to my own question. I just said a mouthful, getting him hip to my game. He was never someone I could look at being in a relationship with. Call me what you want, but you won't be calling me the man that loved another man. I just used what was presented to me to get what I wanted.

"I hear you, Darnell. I hear you loud and clear." For some reason, when he said that to me, the hair on the back of my neck stood up.

Chills ran down my spine, almost causing me to ask him what was up with him.

Notice that I said "almost caused me to ask" and the only reason I didn't was because I was too afraid to ask. He seemed to be on some *Fatal Attraction* type shit and I wasn't trying to be the next victim to his madness. Being that we worked together, there was no doubt in my mind that he wasn't trained to go, but I didn't want to be the target when his ass aimed.

"Cameron, pull over, man," I stated to him. I was being cautious and really needed to get this out in the open to avoid having to have this conversation again.

When he finally veered over to the side of the road, I knew it was now or never. He was holding onto something that was never going to be between the two of us and I had to put an end to it before things got out of hand. That's if it hasn't already.

Turning to look at him, I tried to be as gentle as possible when letting him down. I knew it would be harder than I thought, but I couldn't play around on this any longer. My life was already turned upside down with the way things were working out with Kat and me.

"Before you say anything, let me talk," Cameron said to me. It almost confused me the way he was talking.

"Well, can it wait until I get out what I have to say?"

"No, it can't wait. I've constantly put my feelings on the back-burner for you and I can no longer do it. Especially since you're making it clear that you have no intentions of being with me, which I think is foul. You should never use a person for your own selfish reasons."

I knew he was right when he was saying that. Hell, I didn't know his mental state. I could've driven him over the edge. And if he was already there, I could've caused him to fuck some things up behind me. None of this was looking good for your boy.

❧ 18 ❧

Cameron

"Go ahead and say what you need to say. I can't wait to get out what's on my mind," Darnell stated to me, seeming so nonchalant about what was going on between us.

"From the first time I laid eyes on you, I wanted you. When I had the chance to be with you, I made my move. Needless to say, you enjoyed us having sex as much as I did or we wouldn't be here. We rocked together hard for a while until you decided to find your 'Precious Kat'. You didn't consider any of my feelings in this. It felt like you threw me away like yesterday's trash."

"That was never my intention. But, I'm not into guys like that at all. You were my first experience. The fact that you were a male had nothing to do with me sleeping with you. It was really the fact that I wanted to do anal sex and not many women were willing to try it because of the size of my dick."

"So, you're saying that you used me? Go ahead and just say that instead of beating around the bush. Yeah, it may sound bad, but at least I'll know where we stand."

"I don't think I was using you per se. I think we were both doing something that two consenting adults wanted to do to give us pleasure, but one of us messed around and caught feelings."

"Think whatever you want that'll make you feel better Darnell, but you used me. All these women you call yourself dating have all been tired, thrifty, and through. But things with us have always run smoothly, so why not see where it can go?"

"Cameron, get this through your head; I'm not into dating men. I want a woman. I want a family, so she can be my WIFE and we can have KIDS," he loudly stated, putting emphasis on the words wife and kids.

"We can have a family. You act like same-sex marriages aren't legal these days. And we can adopt kids or pay for a surrogate," I truthfully asserted, meaning every word of what came out of my mouth.

"Naw, we can't. You can do what you want to do, but it won't be involving me."

"I killed somebody over your punk ass and this is the thanks I get? You're one ungrateful son of a bitch."

"What the fuck did you just say?" As soon as he said that, I clasped my hand against my mouth. Not even I could believe I just admitted to what I did.

Sitting there with a stunned expression on my face, I didn't know what to do. I had no choice but to tell him everything. It wasn't like he was going to be with me anyways.

"Do you remember all those letters, texts, and phone calls you were getting?"

"Yeah, but what does that have to do with you?"

"I knew Afreeca before you met her. She's actually a distant cousin of mine that I messed around with from time to time when I just wanted to be with a woman."

"So, when you had a desire to feel a woman, you would sleep with Afreeca? Did you have feelings for her?"

"No, not at all. Like I said, it was only when I desired to be with a woman."

"Let me just be clear with this. You had sex with someone of the opposite sex when you felt like dipping into her treasure box, but you in no way, shape, form or fashion had feelings for her?"

"Bruh, I already told you I didn't. She knew what was up when we started messing around."

"Point proven!" he blurted out to me.

"What are you talking about Darnell?" I anxiously probed.

"You did the same exact thing that I did, but you got mad when it was done to you. I slept with you because you were there. That's the same exact thing you did to this Afreeca girl. But that's neither here nor there, so continue with your story."

I had to admit that he got me. I never thought about what he was saying. I just knew that it showed me as being a hypocrite. That further let me know that he wasn't going to be with me. Who was I kidding to even think that was going to happen in the first place?

Continuing my story, "The night you asked about hanging out, I hit her up. She was single and tired of running into losers. I told her that I had the perfect guy for her and told her about you. That night, we put Rohypnol in your drink, knowing it would knock you out. When we got back to your house, we staged it to look like only you and her had been together, but I was involved the minute the clothes started coming off."

"Do you know that shit is like y'all raped a nigga?" he shouted. Again, something I didn't think about. Damn, yo boy was messing up left and right and didn't even know it. Love will have you doing the most, huh?

"You were all into it, so don't even trip. I need you to let me finish."

"Continue...."

"We started talking about the plans I had in store for you. She was pissed about the way things were going. See, I had her sending you letters and blowing up your phone with the calls and texts, letting you think that she was about to have your child. I told her that you loved children so that would be the best way for her to reel you in. The only thing was that she was throwing the bait out there, but your ass wasn't catching it because of Kat being in the way."

"Wait, so are you about to tell me that you killed Kat? That's exactly where this seems like this is going and if that's the case, then you won't ever see the light of day again and it surely won't be because you're behind prison walls," he snapped. Only this time, he got out of the car and started pacing back and forth. All of this shit was surreal to me. I couldn't believe that things were going left this damn fast.

"No, I didn't kill her. Let me finish!" I angrily demanded. I was tired of him cutting me off. It was only making me more and more frustrated. The fact that he thought it was even okay for him to continue to interrupt me, was not helping the situation. I should've kept this secret to myself. I just knew he was going to make me kill his ass too.

❧ 19 ☙

K ateshia
I woke up smiling down at the way I'd messed with Tavares last night. The fact that the weather was so bad only added more to the dramatics of what I did.

See, I went back to the house that night when Michael was sleep, so I could put a tracker on the car Tavares was driving that I couldn't put on there earlier that day. While I was there, it was thundering and lightening so bad that Tavares took his scary ass on up to the bedroom. I knew from earlier that he had to go out to meet his connect, Rock, so I wouldn't have much time to do what I needed to do.

After I got inside the garage to put the tracker under the car, I went back inside the house to find Tavares. I was very careful with my movement. The lights were out all over the lower level of the house, so I had to remember where everything was. I didn't want to bump into anything or anyone. Knowing Tavares, when the weather got bad, he sent everyone home. Hell, even his scary ass wasn't going to stay in that house by himself.

When I located him, he was upstairs in the room, seemingly packing an overnight bag. I began to spook him by flipping the lights off and on. When they were on, he could see a glimpse of me standing by the lights. I could see him inching closer to me, trying to put his hands on me. When he got a little too close for my enjoyment, I turned the lights off and headed out the door. I ran right back to the car that was parked at the shed and got the hell away from that property.

When I arrived back at home, Michael was also gone. Where he was, I didn't know, but I knew I was going to have to listen to his mouth about me leaving the house again.

The next morning, I rose to the smell of bacon in the air. That just meant that Michael was in the kitchen getting down. That's something I will definitely miss when it's time for me to go; a man being in the kitchen cooking for me. Wouldn't that be something for men to be barefoot in the kitchen cooking and cleaning?

"Mmmm... that smells good," I hungrily stated to him, as I walked up behind him to steal a piece of bacon.

"Dang, somebody being greedy this morning I see. You can't even wait for me to finish cooking?" he asked, chuckling at the sight of me continuing to try to steal more bacon.

"Sorry, I must've worked up an appetite in my sleep."

"You sure it was in your sleep? Maybe it has something to do with the little trip you took while I was sleep."

"Low blow I see. Well, if you must know, I had to go handle something."

"Kat, what the hell is going on? Every time I turn around, you have something to do that you can't let me in on. That shit is mad annoying and is starting to piss me off."

"Well damn Michael! I'm sorry if I don't tell you my every move. As a matter of fact, I think I need to go to the bathroom to take a shit. Do you wanna come help me strain to get it out or roll the tissue out and wipe my ass?"

"Don't be fucking nasty Kateshia. I want to know what the hell is going on. I don't need you getting me involved in no shit like you did Darnell. I love my life and I'm not trying to fight a nigga over no bitch that won't even agree to be with me."

"So, that's how you really feel?" I blurted out, waiting to see what his ass was going to try to say in an attempt to cover up the dumb shit that had just come out of his mouth.

"No, that's not how I feel, but I do feel like you're mentally fucking me," he indicated with frustration in his tone.

I knew that I was the reason behind his frustration. But, I felt like he should understand where I was coming from as well. Michael was very much so a likable person. True, he was sexy, smart, genuine, and trustworthy, which are some of the characteristics I look for in a man, but he also gives me a bad vibe and comes off as being sneaky and a womanizer. Those were the same things I saw in Tavares. I'm not trying to walk away from one quack to be with another. Fuck outta here with that.

"I'm sorry Michael. I do like you, but I just can't be with anyone right now. Not while all of this is going on. Just let me get through this and give me a little time to heal. Then, we can see where things could go with us."

"How much time is that? I've been waiting for years, hell. I'm ready to start a family with you."

"Damn nigga, you don't know me like that. You only know what you've seen from working with me and the things I've told you. Slow your road before you run off it."

Throwing his hands up in defeat, he snatched his keys off the counter and jetted out the house. He didn't bother to turn the food off or put any decent clothes on. Hell, he's a grown man, so he'll be alright. I guess he thought I was the police. Nigga better guess again, shit. I don't get paid to chase and cuff no damn body and I sure as hell wasn't about to pretend I did with his overgrown babyish ass.

I should've told him to take that titty out his mouth and man the fuck up, but I couldn't be too rude with him allowing me to stay in his house. That just let me know that I needed to make things move quicker than what I intended for them to.

After listening to Tavares' conversation, I left a message with an Officer Coleman that I was told had been working closely on my case, informing her of what was about to go down with Tavares and Rock. Hopefully, they set something up to catch his ass when things were going down, so I could come out of hiding. That was at least another charge they could get him with, on top of the one they were going to hit him with for what happened to me.

Now was the time I was dreading. I was going to need some help to set the next parts of my plan in motion. Although I didn't want to, I was going to have to call the one person I dreaded calling the most. I had no choice if I was going to find Darnell and get answers from his scary ass on why he left me the way that he did. All of that was going to have to wait though.

I finished cooking the food Michael stormed out of the house without finishing. Then, I sat my greedy ass right at the table and ate the hell out of the food. I didn't even bother to clean my mess up. I threw everything in the sink and took my happy go lucky ass right on to the room I was staying in to run some bath water and make the call I needed to make. I could feel the lumps forming in my throat as I was dialing the number. Ain't no way in hell I could allow this person to make me so nervous. Fuck it! I'll leave the middle man out and just call his ass myself.

❦ 20 ❦

Darnell

Cameron and I stood on the side of the road for about ten minutes arguing. He admitted to me that he killed someone and, of course, the first thing that came to my mind was that he had killed Kat. I wanted to pounce on him and beat him to death, but that wouldn't get me the answers I wanted. Besides, I needed him alive to go to the police if he was indeed the one responsible for her disappearing.

"Nell, I swear I didn't kill Kat. I had nothing to do with her disappearance. I'm talking about I killed Afreeca. She was planning to expose me to you and take you from me. I couldn't allow that to happen."

"Was she carrying my seed?" I questioned through clenched teeth, growing tired of the bullshit games.

"I don't know if she was pregnant or not. I doubt it because I never saw her go to the doctor and she didn't start talking about being pregnant until I told her to send all those letters to you. So, to answer your question, no, she wasn't pregnant by you or anyone else, for that matter."

I breathed a sigh of relief hearing that. If Kat was alive, then I wouldn't have to worry about hitting her with the crazy baby momma drama. There was still a chance for us to be together and be happy.

Just as I was opening my mouth to say something else to Cameron, my phone started ringing and an unknown number popped up on it. I sent it to voicemail. I didn't have time for that Afreeca chick to be playing any more games on my phone. The minute I had that thought, I had to quickly brush it out of my mind. I had to remember that Cameron just admitted to killing her. I started to wonder what he did to the body. I hadn't heard anything about it on the news, even though I wasn't really paying attention to what was going on due to my focus being solely on Kat.

The phone rang again. It was the same number calling back. I answered it to find out who was so desperately trying to get in touch with me.

"This is Darnell. Who dis?"

"Nell, are you around anyone?" I heard the familiar voice ask. It was music to my ears.

Knowing that she didn't want anyone to know she was talking to me, I simply stated, "I'm with Cameron. What's up?"

"I need to see you now. Is there some place we can meet without someone knowing that I'm with you?"

"I have a room if you want to go there."

"No, that's too out in the open. Get rid of Cameron and turn the location off on your phone. I have somewhere for you to come, but you have to be as discreet as possible about it. The news reporters may be watching your every move, so you need to get here undetected and quick."

After giving me the address, she hung the phone up. Cameron was staring me up and down like he was expecting me to tell him who I was talking to. You know that shit was not about to happen.

"Stop looking at me like that nigga, you not my man. Take me back to my hotel, I need to meet with my attorney."

Cameron looked at me suspiciously, but there was really nothing he could say or do other than to follow my commands. He knew he had torn his ass with me. His freedom was now in my hands. The only way I was going to be free to move on with someone else was to get rid of him, so he better know that this information that I had was going straight to the police when I had things squared away with Kat.

When I made it back to the hotel, I ran up the stairs to my room to freshen up. I checked my surroundings to make sure things were good. When it appeared that everything was clear and I wasn't being watched, I went to my car and searched for any device being placed on it that could lead someone to me. Just as Cameron had stated, he did indeed have a tracking device under my car. I removed it, placed it under my front tire, got in the car, and drove back and forth over the device about five times before putting the address into the GPS on my phone and speeding off.

I continuously surveyed everything that was going on around me. I couldn't wait to get to my baby. I've waited weeks to hold her in my arms again and it was finally about to happen. Then, it suddenly hit me that she was whispering and asked if I was around someone. Why would she want to meet up with me instead of going to the police, so they could no longer declare her missing or dead? Was I being set up? Shit was definitely starting to get real and I'm not sure I was ready for anything else.

Pulling up to the address she gave me, the garage door was open, as she indicated it would be, with a spot for me to park my car. Once I got the car in the garage, the door started to go down behind me and the door leading into the house was open. I had to admit that whoever's house it was, had it on point.

"Kateshia? Where are you?" I called out to her, hoping that it was truly her and nobody trying to play games with me.

"I'm right here," I heard her say from behind me. It scared the shit out of me because I wasn't expecting her to be behind me.

Turning to see her, she was as angelic as she'd always been to me. Nothing was out of place or seemed bruised on her. I rushed over to her, trying to shower her with hugs and kisses, but she threw her hand up to stop me.

"What the fuck?" I turned my nose up at her, wondering what the hell she did that for.

"Watch your step playa, you left me when I needed you the most and I want to know why," she seriously quizzed. There was not an ounce of softness in her face at all. The shit was fucking with me big time. That was a side of her I wasn't used to seeing.

"Kat, I promise it's not what you think. I didn't leave you so that you could get hurt. When I saw you handling business beating the hell out of Tavares, I left. I wasn't thinking straight."

"That's no excuse Nell. I was free. I could've left the house and not looked back, but your ass was still in the basement. That prompted me to stay there to make sure you were okay. Last time I checked, the man was supposed to protect the woman. But you must have a pussy between your legs because you hauled ass, the first chance you got."

Everything she said to me was the truth. I hated that things turned out the way that they did between us, but it was very evident that after everything that happened, there was no coming back from this. She was never going to give me another chance to make things right between us.

"I felt betrayed. I would've never done that shit to you, Darnell. You were wrong on so many levels. After what happened between us in high school, we should've just left well enough alone. It just wasn't meant for us to be and I understand that now."

"You're absolutely right; it wasn't meant for y'all to be," I heard a voice state from behind me.

Turning to look around, there was no one there. I know I wasn't imaging things.

"Who's there?" I shouted out, waiting for a response.

"Kateshia, Kat, or whatever your name is. You don't know me, but I've heard so much about you. I'm glad you're smart enough to realize that Darnell and you will never make it. And trust me dear, it has nothing to do with the fact that he left you to die, but everything to do with the fact that he's gay."

I could hear Cameron talking, but I couldn't see him. I moved throughout the foyer of the house where we were standing, stunned at what I was hearing.

"Cameron, quit playing these games. Get your ass out here now."

"Didn't I tell you to come alone? You're going to get me caught up in some shit before I'm ready to reveal that I'm alive!" Kateshia screamed at me. She appeared to be panicky and her face was looking flustered.

"If you're looking for me, then don't. You won't find me anywhere near wherever you are."

"Then, how the hell are you even talking right now?" I queried, still checking my surroundings for any sign of him.

"Well, dumbass, you must've dialed my number and didn't realize it. I wasn't going to say a word because I wanted to know who you were really going to meet and why you had to be so secretive about it. I knew it wasn't your attorney because you had no problem with me being in his presence earlier."

"Hold the fuck up, you're gay?" Kat shockingly inquired.

"Kat, it's not what you think!' I tried to explain.

"Oh, it is very much so what you think. Darnell likes diving into men just as much as he likes women. However, I do feel he could lean more towards men when it comes to putting it down in the bedroom."

"Cameron, I'm warning you to shut the hell up!"

"Is this Cameron guy, the one you said was your partner? And how would he even know if you were gay or not?"

"Well, since you asked dear, I'm definitely that Cameron that he works with. And the reason I know that he's gay is because he's been dicking me down for some years now. You're not the only one that can get little ole Darnell. He was mine way before you came back into the picture."

There was nothing left for me to say. I just stood there. Cameron just handed my ass to me in front of Kat. I was boiling mad at the way things were going down. I knew I wasn't going to get her back after what happened that dreaded night, but this just further confirmed what I knew. Cameron definitely fucked my chances up of ever being with Kat again. For that, he was going to pay.

"What the fuck is going on in my house?" I heard another male voice state, causing me to turn around in panic. Here we go again with some more bullshit.

21

Michael

Leaving the house for a while was the only way I could keep from putting hands on Kat. She'd pissed me off to the point of no return. Being on the verge of putting hands on her was a point I never thought I'd be at. Seemingly, there was no winning with her. I knew she didn't look at me in the same manner that I looked at her, so why was I going through all this trouble to make her mine? Stupid, huh?

When I got home, I pulled in front of the house, instead of going into the garage. I was planning to run in to get dressed for work, then head back out. In case you're wondering, yes, I was still running Kat's company for her. I should've ran it through the ground, then started my own company and pulled her authors over with me. That was something I couldn't find in my heart to do to her, knowing how hard she worked for it.

Walking inside the house, I could hear screaming and shouting. I knew I left Kat in the house by herself; now, I was hearing two males with her. I knew damn well she didn't have another man in my house. Peeping around the corner where they were standing, I recognized that

Darnell character from pictures that were posted of him on the news when Kat first went missing, but I didn't see the other male.

"What the fuck is going on in my house?" I solicited. I was about to tear some shit up if she was fucking the next nigga in my shit, but wasn't giving the goods up to me.

"Michael, I wasn't expecting you to return so soon," Kat said like there was nothing wrong with another man being in my house.

"What the hell do you mean you didn't expect me to return so soon? You know I left to cool off. Why would I not come back to the place that I pay bills at?"

"That's not what I meant Michael. You know what, I'm not doing this with you. You've been an ass to me ever since you realized you weren't getting any pussy."

"Don't nobody want that ole dry ass pussy," I lied. I said that to damage her ego when the truth was, I wanted her more than a homeless person wanted a home.

"She's far from dry nigga. And you won't be talking to her like that in my presence."

"Did I ask you to say anything to me? Her credit is good right now; I'll let your bitch ass know when she needs a cosigner."

This nigga was really pushing his luck with me. I wasn't the type of nigga that was going to let someone disrespect me in my home. He may have pulled that shit in Tavares' house, but he was not about to do that in mine.

"Darnell, help me get my things, I have to get out of here. My dry pussy and I'll gladly go somewhere that doesn't have crybaby ass niggas floating around." I knew that was her way of throwing a shot at me, but that didn't even matter. What mattered was her getting the hell out of my crib before I killed them all.

"Where do you think you're going? I hope to the police station to let them know you're okay before I go for you."

"You wouldn't dare go to the police. What exactly are you going to tell them? That you knew I was missing, but you still decided to let me stay at your house, instead of telling them that I was alive?"

"How are they supposed to know that you've been here? You're about to go into hiding again."

"Remember the phone you gave me? When they trace it back, it'll show up that you purchased it, as well as the card that you loaded money on. And if Tavares was smart enough to check the cameras from the house, they can clearly see me driving past in one of your vehicles."

"Are you threatening me, Kat?"

"Oh, not at all Michael; I'm only returning the guarantee of going to the police that you just gave to me. Don't do me if you don't want me to do you!"

I could see then, that this bitch was not worth the trouble I had to deal with. Her mouth was too damn smart and her attitude was utterly ridiculous. I see now why Tavares stayed whipping up on her ass. I would've done the same thing if I was married to her or even dated her for as long as he did.

"Fine, get the hell out my shit. I don't have to deal with this shit from you or any other bitch. You're not worth any of the shit that I've done. But you better know that this won't be the last time your ass hears from me."

"Oh, I'm sure this isn't the last time I hear from your dick beating ass. Something's been off about you for a while now. If I find out that you had anything to do with any of this, you'll have hell to pay." She turned and walked to the direction of the room that she was staying in.

I was glad she was leaving. It would give me time to revamp my plan in regards to her. The first plan didn't work out the way I'd hoped, due to someone being careless. The fact that she chose to come to me when she broke free made me think she was showing an interest in me or, in the least, that she trusted me, but she just showed her true colors. Kat hadn't saw the last of me, and soon, she would find that out.

22

Lateshia

After Mrs. Scott left my house, my dad and I felt some type of relief, but we knew that I still wasn't out of the woods. Instead of going to the doctor that same day, we headed straight to Dr. Hines office the first thing this morning. I was hella nervous sitting there waiting for them to call my name. As Mrs. Scott stated, when I told them what I was there for, it really didn't take them much time to call me to the back. I was ready for this to all be over with.

The lady drew blood from me, I gave a urine sample, and then I was escorted into an examination room. When the nurse came in, she told me to undress from the waist down and place a sheet over myself. My father stayed in the room while I completed the task. I knew the nurse must've thought I was crazy, but hell, he had seen it anyways, so what difference did it make?

"I see it's still as pretty as it's always been," he commented to me, making me blush. I knew I couldn't go there with my father again, so I chose not to even respond to what he was saying.

Smiling, I laid back on the table awaiting Dr. Hines's entrance into the room. Once she walked in there, it was as if you could cut the tension with a knife. She tried to plaster a smile on her face, but I already knew it was fake. In fact, the more she looked at me, the more I could remember seeing her face somewhere outside of the doctor's office. If I didn't know any better, I'd say that I may have screwed her husband. That could be why she was coming at me the way she was. Doctor or not, she was still any other bitch in my eyes.

"How are you doing today, Lateshia?" she politely asked, which really shocked the hell out of me. *Look at her trying to be all professional. Ain't no way in hell I would be in a situation like this trying to be the bigger woman. Let a bitch come in my clinic and I realize she done slept with my husband, I'd ram those clamps straight up her cat,* I thought to myself.

Giggling to myself, I found the time to stop and respond, "I'm fine Dr. Hines. Ready to get this over with; how are you today?"

"I'm doing quite well, thanks for asking. And I can see why you would want to get something like this over with. I hate that we had to send the worker from the health department out to your house, but that is the protocol when we think someone may have an STD and we can't get ahold of them."

"That's completely understandable. If anything, I just want to know for sure, so that I will know how to proceed with my life."

"I can agree with you wanting to know. How about we have your father step out so that we can move right along with getting this procedure done? The results I can give you in the office will be for HPV, Trichomonas, Chlamydia, and Gonorrhea. Your blood will be sent to the lab to be tested for Syphilis, Herpes, Hepatitis, and HIV. Do you understand that?"

"Yes, I do understand, and there is no need to send my father out the room. He's sitting up by my head, so he can't see anything. I need him in here for support."

"While it's not a common thing unless you were a minor, I'll move forward with your wishes as soon as my nurse returns to the room."

The nurse came back inside the room roughly five minutes later. It didn't bother me that it took her a minute to return, but it appeared to have agitated Dr. Hines. It may've had something to do with the fact that we were sitting in the exam room for what seemed like a long period of time in complete silence.

The nurse finally came in acting all preppy, like there was really something to be happy about. I wanted to smack the smile off her face, but I didn't. I just laid there and prayed that my body was healthy and I'd be fine.

I couldn't get out the clinic fast enough. For a minute, I forgot that my father was with me. I sped down the freeway heading back to my house. The minute I got there, I went straight to my room without making sure my father was in the house.

"Are you okay Lat?" he asked on the opposite side of my bedroom door. I knew he was only showing concern for me, but I didn't want to be bothered by anyone. My sister was missing, I didn't know for sure if I was pregnant or not, my mother was no longer talking to me due to my indiscretions with my father, and now I may have a deadly disease.

"What else can you do to punish me?" I looked up, shouting at God. I know you aren't supposed to question him, but who else was going to answer my questions?

"Well, for starters, I could beat that ass," a female voice returned to me. Oh, hell naw, I got up and headed for the door. I knew no one was supposed to be home but my father and me, so the fact that I heard another voice was some straight up freaky shit. There was no way I was about to stick around and find out where it was coming from.

Just as I made it to the door, I was grabbed from behind. I started swinging wildly, trying to get whoever it was to release me. Any attempts of me trying to scream were muffled by them placing their hands over my mouth.

"Open the door Lateshia. What is going on in there?" My father started pounding on the door and twisting the doorknob, trying to get to me.

"I'm fine dad. I saw a bug, but it's gone now," the voice responded. Gradually, I stopped swinging.

"Kateshia?" I heard my father state.

"No dad, it's Lateshia," she returned to him. But, just like me, he was no fool. My father knew my sister's voice just as well as I did.

When she let me go, I turned around and pulled her in for a hug. Tears were running down both of our faces. I didn't want to let her go. I just knew for sure that Tavares had killed her.

"I'm so sorry Kateshia. I'm so very sorry. I shouldn't have done the things that I did to you. You didn't deserve it. I was so jealous of you. I always thought you were being shown favoritism by mom and dad and I never understand why. But I was wrong, I was so wrong," I rambled on until she slapped fire out of me.

"What the hell did you do that for? I just apologized to you," I cried out, grabbing my cheek that was still stinging from being hit.

"I understand that you apologized, but that doesn't change the fact that you tried to destroy my life. I never would've done that to you. But right now is not the time for us to get into this. We'll sit down and talk about this in due time. Right now, I have bigger fish to fry and I need your help to do so."

"Whatever you need me to do, I'm down. I just want my sister back. You were my best friend and I never realized how much I should've valued you until I no longer had you in my life. Please tell me that we can work on us," I begged, damn near wanting to drop to my knees to show her that I was sincere in what I was saying.

"Let's not talk about this right now. Are you going to help me or are you going to continue to babble about something I said we could talk about later?"

I was shocked by the way Kat was handling me. She used to act so timid and scared, although I knew she had a lot of fight in her. Instead on continuing to try to apologize like I felt the need to do, I was prepared to help. My sister needed me for a change and I wasn't going to disappoint her.

"What do you need me to do sis?"

"Just call me Kateshia or Kat until we have our little talk," she hurriedly changed my wording. I wanted to pluck her eyebrows out, but I knew better.

"That's fine Kat. What do you need me to do?"

"Come on, we have to get out of here and I'll explain everything to you."

I stood there for a while before moving. I didn't want to say this, but I felt like Kat was gearing up to take me somewhere and beat my ass for betraying her. That thought alone made me cautious of trying to go anywhere with her.

"I'm not about to play with you, Lat. Either you're coming or you ain't. I'm not setting you up to do anything to you. This is all about Tavares and the hell he has put me through. It's time for him to pay the piper."

The look of rage in her eyes was all the confirmation I needed to know she was aiming for him and not me. She didn't have to tell me twice. I was on my way to help my sister get revenge, not only for her, but for me as well. She may not know it, but I believe I was going to get more joy out of hurting Tavares than she would.

23

avares

Trying to get as far away from the warehouse as I could, I headed to the nearest hotel. There was no way I could go back to the house when I was as paranoid as I was. Some shady shit was going down and I wanted to know what it was.

Needing to get my thoughts together, I was more than ready to relax and dip into something wet. Not wanting to call anyone that would be all in my business or run their mouth, I decided that Andrea was my best bet. She bit my dick the last time I had a sexual encounter with, her but from the way I hemmed her up, I'm sure she'd learned her lesson.

Me: Sup Drea! What's up with you?

Drea: Not too much. I'm just lounging around the house trying to decide if I want to go out with the girls tonight or not.

Me: How about you come hang with me tonight? I'll make it worth your while.

Drea: Aight cool. Where you wanna meet at?

Me: Meet me at the Barksdale Hotel. I'm not trying to have my business all in the streets.

Drea: K. I'll be there in an hour.

The moment she said she was going to kick it with your boy, a nigga was grinning from ear to ear. I hadn't had sex in forever and was ready to beat her back in and make her damn knees buckle. She just didn't know what she was about to get herself into.

After checking in the room, I sent Drea a text, letting her know the room number and headed straight to the room. An eerie feeling fell upon me, making me think some shit was about to go down. I couldn't afford for anything else to go wrong right now.

As I was preparing myself to get in the shower before Drea arrived, I could hear my phone ringing. I answered it without looking at the caller id, even though I wasn't in the mood to be bothered by anyone.

"Yo, who is it?"

"Hey Tavares, it's Lateshia," she happily stated.

"What the hell do you want? Didn't we just have an altercation and I told you to stay away from me?"

"Yeah, but I miss you. I gotta have you inside of me now," she was pleading for me to plunge inside of her.

My eyebrows raised and I began to think of the possibilities of having two ladies together.

"Is that right? How bad do you want it?"

"I want it bad daddy. So, bad that I want you to dig my ass out too."

Damn, she was sounding freaky as hell and I couldn't resist what she was offering. Lateshia got on my nerves, but she had some bomb ass head and her pussy stayed sloppy wet. There was no way I was going to pass on the chance to murder her pussy again.

"Okay, I'm at the Barksdale Hotel room 611. Come get it. But, don't bother showing up if you're not prepared for anything because it's definitely about to go down here."

"I hear you talking Courvoisier. Let me freshen up and I'll be there as soon as possible."

"Aight. Bet!"

By the time I hung the phone up, I had one foot already in the shower. I dropped my phone down on the rug that was in the bathroom. Luckily, it was in an otter box because I would've snapped if I ended up cracking my screen.

For some reason, I began rapping and dancing while I was in the shower. The thought of having a threesome tonight was making things look up for me.

Fuck a shooter, I'm my own shooter. All this ice, I'm my own jeweler. Six lawyers and they're all Jewish. I'm the star, bitch this my movie.

Plies ain't no damn joke with those lyrics. Made me wish I would've taken my ass to the Ritz-Carlton for what was about to go down in this room. Oh well, as long as I was about to get it in, I wasn't going to complain.

As I felt the water getting cold, I knew it was time for me to get out the shower. Just as I was about to wrap the towel around my body, I could hear someone knocking on the door. I knew it was either Lat or Drea. It didn't matter who it was to me because we were about to get it popping before the other one arrived. When I opened the door, I was stunned to see who it was.

24

*K*ateshia

I'm sure people are thinking I'm dumb for depending on my sister at a time like this, when all she's done was betray me, but I was far from it. I needed her to help me make things work with Tavares.

The moment she agreed to help, I had her get our father's attention and take him to the kitchen, so I could sneak out through the living room to her car. Then, she came out to the car and took off while I laid low in the backseat.

We got a hotel room at the Days Inn, in my friend, Destinee's, name. That room became our new meeting spot. Darnell had a cab drop him off at a store nearby and waited a while before Lat and I scooped him up.

There I was in the presence of two more people who'd hurt me, but don't worry, I was going to get the last laugh when it came to both of those bastards, too. Getting back to the hotel room, they stared at each other, as if they were ready to attack one another at any minute.

"Let's go ahead and get this out the way before we go any further. There is clearly tension in the room between the two of ya'll. I'm not sure if you're scared that I'm going to beat your ass or if you just can't stand each other."

"Kat, what does this have to do with anything? I thought we were here to help you take care of Tavares," Lat stated, seeming appalled at what I was saying to them.

"I'm getting to all of that, but both of you are going to hear me out right now." There was complete silence in the room. When I knew I'd gained their undivided attention, I proceeded to talk.

"Now, Lat, you were my sister and best friend. We were twins, so we should've felt each other's pain, if you ask me. Whenever you needed me, there wasn't a time that I wasn't there for you. Just because we went in different directions with our lives doesn't give you the right to call yourself trying to hate me and destroy anything I wanted for myself."

"I guess I should tell you something since we're talking about this now. I was diagnosed with Schizophrenia a while back, but I never told anyone. In my head, things are one way, but they really aren't what they seem. I'm not saying that as an excuse, but I just want you to know that I have mental issues. And once this is over, I would like to let you in on a lot of other major things that are going on with me."

"Oh, I've always knew your ass was nuttier than a ball sac, but I never said anything because you were my sister and I loved you. Despite your flaws, I overlooked everything that you've done in the past and still accepted you. But, it's okay Lat. I know that I can't live my life holding grudges against you. You just further proved that you can't even trust family."

Knowing that it wasn't healthy to hold grudges, I was going to forgive her. But, I'd never forget what she did to me. If she thought we were going to be best friends again, then she had another thing coming. The whole time we were talking, I could see that Darnell was becoming uneasy, thinking what I would say to him or if I would expose him. I wouldn't even waste my breath breaking him down that way. He had his own demons, wanting to be with people of the same sex, and he was going to have to deal with it. If that's what made him happy, then more power to him. I just knew that there was no chance in hell of us getting back together again.

"You can relax Nell; we already talked earlier and concluded that we could never be. No matter what your excuse was for leaving me there with Tavares, there was no way in hell a real man would've left his woman to fend for herself against a man twice her size."

"Well, I still want to apologize for the way I hurt you. I truly am sorry for the way that things went down. If I could take things back, then I would."

"It's all good. The only thing you can do for me now is work on yourself and figure out what you're going to do about your situation. And at some point, the two of you are going to have to talk through what happened between y'all."

"We actually already talked about it and I do owe you an apology. I wasn't a virgin when we first had sex Darnell. I only told you that because I really liked you and thought that you would value me more, but I was completely wrong. The way things went down between us hurt me, so I tried to make you feel bad by saying you raped me. I know what really happened, but I thought if I made you feel bad, then you would want to be with me."

"Lat, that's bullshit and you know it! If you would've told somebody that and they actually believed you, then I would've been in jail for something I didn't do. Did you even think about that?"

"No, I didn't think about it. I just wanted attention from someone and that was the only way I could think to get it from you. Like I said, I apologize for all the turmoil I caused you all these years."

"Just know that when this is all said and done, we may as well cut ties. Kat and I've already decided to go our separate ways, so there is no reason for us to maintain any contact."

"That's fine with me. You were in my past and I'm more than prepared to leave you there at this point. I have too much stuff going on with me to be worried about what you or anyone else has going on."

"Well, now that we have that all out the way, I would like for us to get down to business regarding Tavares. I know that my time is limited now that I 've shown myself to some people and eventually, people are going to start recognizing me. I have to get things in the works to bring Tavares down before I turn myself in."

"What do you have in mind?" Nell and Lat asked in unison.

"Well, he went to meet with his connect last night. That's some ugly ass banana boat looking nigga named Rock. When he went to meet with him, I tipped the police off on what was going on and called Rock, pretending to be Tavares' secretary, saying he needed to cancel the meeting. I stood by to see what would happen, but Tavares must've detected the heat on him and turned around before making it to the warehouse good.

"I called Rock back to let him know that Tavares was planning on giving him the product back and letting the police know who he was. Rock wasn't too happy about that and wanted to know Tavares' whereabouts. I've watched the house and know that Tavares isn't there, so he must be staying in a hotel. Lat, this is where you come in at."

"What do you need me to do sis?"

I cleared my throat when I heard the word sis come out of her mouth. I could've sworn that I already told her not to call me that. We were nowhere near that point where she could think we were as close as sisters should be, so there was no reason for her to think it was cool to call me sis.

"I'm sorry. What do you need me to do Kat?" Lat corrected herself, appearing a bit shaken that I would make her change what she was referring to me as. Nell sat there the whole time chuckling at our interaction, but I didn't see a damn thing funny. When he saw that I had a serious facial expression, he immediately changed his demeanor and stopped laughing.

"I need for you to call him like you miss him. Tell him that you want to link up with him again because the dick was so good to you and see if he'll let you meet him somewhere. If he asks you to meet at your house, remind him that our parents are in town so you can't go there."

"Okay, sounds simple enough. Then what?" Nell chimed in to say.

"Let's get this part out the way first, then we'll go from there."

I was really grasping for straws. I didn't know where I was really going with this. I wasn't sure if I wanted to let Rock know where Tavares was or if I was going to go handle him myself at this point. Hell, I may even do both. That's if Rock left something for me to do once he got his hands on him.

Lat picked up her phone to call Tavares as requested, making sure to put the phone on speaker so that Nell and I would be able to hear the entire conversation.

"*Yo, who is it?*" Tavares quizzed as his baritone voice blasted through the phone.

"*Hey Tavares, it's Lateshia,*" Lat responded, trying to sound as cheerful as possible.

"*What the hell do you want? Didn't we just have an altercation and I told you to stay away from me?*" Tavares ferociously snapped at Lat. He seemed as though she was bothering him, but I don't know why when he's never turned down the chance to get pussy.

"*Yeah, but I miss you. I gotta have you inside of me now,*" Lat returned, attempting to sound as though she was pleading with him to see her. I whispered to her that she needed to make it seem as though she missed having him inside of her because I knew it would blow his ego up even more.

Tavares paused for a minute, as if he was in deep thought about something. Then, he finally started back talking. "*Is that right? How bad do you want it?*" he questioned, as if he wasn't too sure about her contacting him.

"*I want it bad daddy. So, bad that I want you to dig my ass out too.*" Lat was convincing as hell. For a moment there, the look on her face appeared as though she was recalling a previous time she was with him. It almost upset me, but I let it slide. Next time, I was going to be on her ass like a scab covering a third-degree burn.

But, like I said, Lat sounded very convincing. I wondered if the freakiness she was presenting to him was the thing that made him continuously go after her. It was very evident then that he wasn't going to pass on the chance of hooking up with her, no matter what kind of rift they previously had. I was going to be sure to ask her about it when they got off the phone.

Then, just like a typical thirsty male, Tavares gave up his location to Lat like it was nothing. "*Okay, I'm at the Barksdale Hotel, room 611. Come get it. But, don't bother showing up if you not prepared for anything because it's definitely about to go down here,*" he comically indicated to her.

It almost made me sick to my damn stomach the way the exchange was going between the two of them. Imagine being me and visualizing your man fucking your sister. Oh yeah, I was definitely going to have to get at both of them for this betrayal.

"I hear you talking Courvoisier. Let me freshen up and I'll be there as soon as possible," was the way Lat commented on what he said to her.

"Aight. Bet!" Tavares stated before ending the call. I told Lat to make sure the phone was hung up before she began talking.

After she did, I called Rock and let him know where Tavares was. I told him not to finish Tavares off because there were some things I wanted to do to him. One of the first things I wanted to do was find out who he was working with. Whoever that bitch was that he had kidnap me was going to see me again. I hope like hell she didn't think I forgot about her.

❧ 25 ❧

ndrea
Little did Kat know, but ever since I'd been out the box, I'd been watching her every move. I wasn't in no way, shape, or form going to turn back now from getting what I wanted, especially when I'd gotten so close to getting it.

In the midst of me watching Kat, I'd been avoiding the person who really asked me to get rid of Tavares. I took her so that Nell and Tavares could both possibly catch a charge behind her. That, to me, would make her look like a hoe with two men on her ass, like they were flies in a flytrap.

I'd been hiding out at a hotel for a while so that no one would be able to find me. That would give me time to get my mind right and come up with a better plan on how to handle Kat. Now that my money was low, I knew I was going to have to go back home to rethink my strategy.

Tavares called me to come pay him a visit at the Barksdale Hotel. I didn't know why he was there or how long he was planning to stay there, but if I could help it, I would be staying there with him. I didn't have the money to continue to pay for my own room and asking him for money was out of the question. So, why not impose on him, since I knew the main reason he was calling me was because he was prepared to smash.

I had to make a stop by my house on the way to see Tavares, so that I could switch my clothes and freshen up. The minute I walked in my house and turned the lights on, I began to scream. The person that I was trying to avoid was now sitting inside my living room with a mug on his face. I knew he wanted to charge me right then, but he also wanted to know what happened.

"He-y-y-y-y," I stuttered. This nigga had me off my A-game, which was unusual for me.

"Hey hell, that shit is for horses. You have to be a fuckin' idiot to allow her to put your dumb ass in a box."

"I know. I don't know what came over me. She was saying all this-" Without giving me time to explain, I was smacked clean across the room. "Please don't hit me again," I pleaded while holding my now bruised face. I could feel the swelling already starting.

"Don't say shit. I have to think. You've ruined everything. I can't allow you to live. She's seen your face and knows that you're connected to what happened to her."

"No, you have it all wrong."

"Didn't I tell you not to say shit? I don't have anything wrong. Say it again and you'll be eating your words."

"Okay, okay, just please hear me out. Yea, she's seen me, but she knows nothing about me. Besides, there's no way for her to link me to you. So, you don't have to kill me after all," I was practically begging for my life at this point.

How the hell could I do this to myself? I should've never agreed to get involved in no dumb shit like this. My mother warned me that this would backfire on me, but looking at the money and the chance to actually make Tavares my man was intriguing to me. I allowed the glitz and glamour of this thrill to get the best of me.

Now, I'm on this cold floor regretting ever getting involved with this man. I just knew trying to plead for my life right now was no use.

"No, baby sis, that's where you're wrong," my big brother wickedly stated to me while he paced back and forth on the vinyl flooring, almost kicking up chunks of vinyl the way his feet were hitting against it.

"See, you have no backbone and just like everyone else in our family, you're only going to look out for yourself. What does that mean you ask? Well, baby sis, if Kat goes to the police and identifies you, which she is capable of doing, they will arrest you. Once they arrest you, you're going to sing like a humming bird and identify me as your partner in crime. I'm sure you've heard that snitches get stitches and end up in ditches. Well, I prefer to go ahead and lay you down before you even get the chance to tell on me."

"Noooooo... I promise I won't tell a single soul. I'll even leave town right now. That'll keep anyone from linking us together. But, please let me live. I'm pregnant!"

"Bitch please! I know you can't get pregnant."

"Well, I have a mental issue."

"Oh, that you definitely have. But, that's still no reason to keep you here on Earth."

"But I'm your sister. Doesn't that mean anything at all to you?"

"You're my half-sister, so no; it doesn't mean a thing to me. We've never even had a real relationship. You're just now starting to talk to me because you wanted something in return. If I never would've told you that I could get you involved with a baller, then you wouldn't have dare dealt with me as long as you have."

"That's not true Bear. You know that I've always looked up to you. I'm telling you, I'll leave town. That way, they won't be able to find me. She doesn't know my name, she has no pictures of me, hell, she can't even remember where she knows me from. If she was going to go to the police, then she would've gone by now and this missing person's case would've quickly became a kidnapping case."

"You don't know her the way that I do. Her thought process is not like the rest of us, so you don't know what she has up her sleeve. Just because she hasn't gone to the police yet, doesn't mean that she isn't."

"Well, let me at least continue to be your inside person when it comes to dealing with Tavares. I can still keep you informed on what's going on with the investigation since you can't actually talk to him or the police about it yourself. We have to be able to work something out."

He stood there as if he was thinking about what I'd just said to him. I prayed I'd given him enough to think about, that was sensible enough for him to let me live.

The only thing I could do was stay on Tavares's good side, so I could get information about Kat to feed to Bear. But, for some reason, I couldn't understand Tavares or my brother. It seemed to me that they made like they were so interested in catching Kat one minute and the next minute, they were like "Man, fuck Kat!' Nobody had time for the back and forth, especially if it could eventually play a role in me finally getting my relationship with Tavares.

Being sick of the whole situation, I was more than ready for all this bullshit to end. Tavares called me to come over and I was on my way to do just that before Bear showed his ass up here trying to take over things. When all of this was said and done, Michael would never have to worry about seeing or hearing from me again.

❦ 26 ❧

Michael
      Nobody will ever understand how much Kat meant to
      me. I've wanted her from the very first time I laid eyes on
her, but Tavares was making it difficult for me to get to her. I could
recall the first time she walked into the publishing company I used to
work at.

*Rogers and Rogers Publications was a small publishing company that took
on a lot of assistants because although they were small, they were the most experienced publishers in the state. People would kill for the chance to get hired by
the company. That was mostly due to being guaranteed a job if they could handle
their work.*

*Kat walked in wearing a black pencil skirt and a black and white polka dot
blouse with some black pumps that defined her calves. Her body was bad, but
that wasn't what caught my eye. She looked angelic and innocent. It was very
obvious that she was smart by the conversation she was able to carry.*

*The moment I realized she was an author, I had my boss assign anything
dealing with her books to me. I figured that would be a great way for me to close
to her. But, no matter what I did to win her over, she always threw up Tavares
and the fact that she was so in love with him. That prompted me to start*

following him around to see what he was about, and just as I suspected, that nigga wasn't about shit.

Don't get me wrong. I'm not a man that wants to see another man fall short, but in that instance, it would've worked out in my favor. I would take pictures of him in awkward positions with other women and leave them around for Kat to find. Still, she continued to love him and go through the motions of trying to maintain her relationship with him. It started to make her look pathetic in my eyes.

The thought of her staying with someone, knowing that he was constantly hurting her, drove me insane. If I could shake her and get her to wake up to the idea of there being someone better out there for her, then I would have. However, something kept telling me that, no matter what, she was going to stick by her man.

Now, in my opinion, there ain't that much love in the world, but who was I to tell her who she should and shouldn't love when I was aiming to get her to love me? I had her working late, going to out of town meetings with me, private tutorial sessions; you name it and I bet I did it, but none of that worked with her. It wasn't until she called me to help out in her firm that I came up with the big idea to get my sister involved.

Andrea was my half-sister. She'd never really been about much, other than trying to find another way to come up. Telling her about Tavares was great for me because I knew she'd want to sink her teeth into him as quickly as possible. To her, he was a boss nigga; to me, he wasn't shit. She wanted Tavares just from me talking about him, so as the loving big brother that I was, my goal was to help her get him.

"Hey Drea! What's been going on with you?"

"Nothing at all Bear. I hear you've taken on a new job."

"I guess your mother told you, huh? Well, it's just a temporary gig to help a friend out. Maybe she'll like what I do around there and keep me around permanently."

"That'd be great. I know you're amazing at what you do, so she'd be a fool not to keep you around."

"You are shole right about that sis." Then, there was silence on the line. See, Andrea may've been my half-sister, but we didn't really get down like that. We would talk here and there, but it was nothing really major. In fact, the only

reason we'd really know what was going on with each other is if our parents told us. By the way, our parents would be either her mother or our father, who also happens to be a hoe. But that's another story for a different day.

"So, what do I owe the pleasure of this call?"

"Well, I know a guy that's in an unhappy marriage that's looking for someone to hang out with. He has a lot of money and he's a big-time attorney. In fact, you may already know who I'm talking about."

"And who might that be?"

"Tavares Jordan."

"Oooooo, I know exactly who you're talking about. He stays on the news defending people, even if there's evidence stacked against them. He's fine as hell, but I don't know about him. He seems shady."

"He may be a little shady, but what attorney do you know that isn't? And it's not like we don't all lie at some time or another."

"Nigga, I don't lie. You know I always keep shit 100."

"Drea, stop the madness. Your ass over there lying now!"

"I have no idea what you're talking about," she tried to play it off. But, I could hear her ass laughing through the phone.

"Well, since you don't know what I'm talking about, let me help jog your memory. Remember the time the woman with the prosthetic leg and wooden teeth found out you were sleeping with her man? She was telling everybody that she was going to take her leg off and beat your ass with it. You talked all that shit about what you were going to do, then the minute you were face-to-face with her, you tried to deny everything. Looks like a lie to me. Oh, and let's not forget the time that you-"

"Shut the hell up Bear; your ass always trying to bring up old shit, ole shabby ass nigga. Get on my damn nerves trying to bring up the past," she said, cutting me off and not allowing me to finish calling her out on her bullshit.

I knew she was pissed off, which is why I started laughing at her. She was too much for herself. "I was just trying to refresh your mind on a few things."

"Nigga, I don't need you to refresh anything over here, unless you planning on running a hose through this drain to unstop it."

Now, I know what you're probably thinking. But don't! I ain't ever touched her ass a day in my life. She walked in on me and saw me naked a few times and has always tried to get at me, but I'm not trying to be talked about or walk around with deformed children. She can miss me with that shit.

"Not happening. I swear the thirst is real with you. Do you want in on him or not?"

"And what's in this for you? You never try to put someone on to something, unless you're going to get something out of it." That, she was telling the truth about.

"You are correct sis. He's in an unhappy marriage to the woman I know I would be happy with. She's the one, sis, and I know it. I just need you to run interference with him so that I can be with her."

"Bear, do you really think this woman is going to leave her husband to run off in the sunset with your demented ass?" She tried it by trying to question my intelligence.

"What the hell did you mean by that? I'm a great man," I screamed through the phone, feeling my body starting to heat up. If she was in my presence, she'd probably have been a dead duck. Fuck does she think she's talking to like that?

"I'm just saying Bear; you aren't exactly an honest man, no matter how you try to portray yourself. You toss away the women who want you and go through hell to get the women who're taken. Who in their right mind does that?"

"You don't know what the hell you're talking about Andrea. Either you're going to step in and start breaking this nigga off to get his mind off his wife or I'm just going to find someone else to do it. Besides, you aren't even looking at the big picture to all of this. You act like you my bitch."

"I could be, but you playing!" Did her dumb ass just say that to me?

"You're my sister! I don't know how many times I can tell your ass that. It's not happening. Get on board or get left behind," I scolded her with so much anger, rage, and resentment in my tone. She just didn't know that I would've snapped her damn neck if I could've.

That phone call sparked the formulation of my plan to get rid of Tavares. Even when that Darnell dude came into the picture, I knew all about him. I knew about the twisted mind games his partner was playing on him too. I was going to use that to my advantage if Kat didn't see him for the clown he was when it was all said and done.

The night that everything went down with Kat, Tavares, and Nell, I was close by watching it all take place. When I realized that Nell had gotten away and Kat was making her way out, I knocked her out and took her to the shed behind their house. I had Drea watch over her for me. The plan was for me to be the one to save her, so she could run into my arms. I knew her relationship with Tavares had been done months ago, and since Nell walked away leaving her to take care of herself, I knew she wouldn't be going back to him either, so that left me. However, Drea let her jealousy issues get the best of her and allowed Kat to get away.

She acted like I don't know she stripped Kat and ate her pussy the first chance she got. I guess she was dying to know what she tasted like. Don't think it didn't cross my mind, but I couldn't violate her like that knowing she would be mine in the end, so I would have free range to play in her treasure chest anytime I wanted to.

The fact that Drea allowed her to get away angered me. I'm not sane when I'm upset, which is what Drea meant when she called me demented. The only reason I'm still allowing her to take breaths was because Kat turned to me for help. I knew she trusted me, which was all I wanted. Once I had her trust, everything else would fall into place.

Now, there I was sitting in my car, holding my pistol and ready to end a few people's lives. My plan had backfired tremendously. I thought I primed Kat to be what I needed her to be, but she'd yet to learn to stay in a woman's place, which was behind her man. I hate to do this, but tonight may be her last day on Earth, too.

Cocking my gun, I fixed the bulge growing in my pants from the mere thought of Kat and readied myself to step out of my car and bust down the door to the hotel room to get my girl. Just as I was about to step my foot outside the door, I could see Kat walking out the hotel with her sister and that Darnell character following closely behind them. I don't know where they were headed, but the minute they hopped inside that Gold Pontiac G6, I was in hot pursuit.

❧ 27 ❧

Darnell

Shit was getting real with Kat and Tavares. She recruited Lat and me to help her get Tavares where she wanted him, so she could pass his ass off to his drug connect. Her goal behind that was to have the man thinking Tavares was about to turn on him. I was down for helping her; I felt I owed her that much.

When we got back to the hotel room, there was so much tension between the three of us. We were at least able to come to an agreement that things weren't what they should've been with either of us and once we got out of this mess we were in, it would be best if we all went our own separate ways. For me, it would be easy to do. It was going to be very complicated for them being that they were sisters, twins at that.

The shit that got me about it all was when Lat went to talking about her mental issues. She acted like no one was aware of her having them, but I been knowing the broad was crazy as hell. She just confirmed it for me. Then, she had the audacity to try to use it as an excuse for her inappropriate behavior. I guess her parents never hipped her to the fact that excuses are the tools of the incompetent; they are used to build monuments of nothingness. That's exactly what her excuses meant to me, nothing.

The only reason I even stuck around after she said what she had to say about what happened between us in high school was because Kat needed us to carry out her plan. If it wasn't for her, you best believe I would've been on the first thing smoking back to Washington.

Now get this, I haven't heard from Cameron since everything that happened at that nigga Michael's house. I still wanted to put hands on him for the way he handled Kat and talked to me out the side of his neck when we were in his presence. I'm a firm believer that if I ain't disrespecting you, then you don't need to be disrespecting me.

"Darnell, are you good with what I just said?" I could hear Kat saying, taking me out of my trance.

"Uh, yeah sure. I'm good with whatever you decide. It's your show Kat," I lied. I didn't hear anything she said. I was too busy thinking about how Lat almost set me up and messed up my life before I even experienced adulthood. I guess I should be thankful that her crazy mind didn't allow her to carry through with it.

"So, what exactly is it that you need me to do Kat?" I curiously queried, since I didn't know what she really said.

"Well, I called Rock, and he's on his way to the hotel to handle Tavares. We need to get there as well to make sure he doesn't kill him. I want him to rot behind bars for all the things he's done. Tonight, everything should be over with and we should be able to carry on with our lives like normal people."

"What are we going to do when we get there?" Lat interrupted to ask.

"Well, we're going to have recorders on all of us and get a full confession out of Tavares. Then, we're going to turn them off and each take a turn whooping his ass until the cops arrive."

"So, what are you going to say when they ask you about your disappearance?" I probed. To me, there was no way around telling them the truth about where she'd been.

"I'm going to tell them exactly what happened. And I'm going to let them know that I couldn't come forward because Tavares would've killed me if I didn't have enough information on him to lock him away for a while."

She looked like she was fearful of something going wrong. To be honest, I was worried that something bad would come of this. Y'all remember the last time her ass came up with a plan that I tried to follow through with. It ended up with us being locked in the basement of her house with my nipples being electrocuted. Chills ran down my back at the thought of that shit happening again.

"Are you sure what you're planning to do is going to work this time? I don't have time to be trapped in basements and dungeons and shit," I hastily stated, meaning every word of it.

"Yes, we're good this time. Like I said, Rock is going to get to him first and put a beating on him, so there really won't be much left for us to do."

"You say that now, but then we get there and things may be completely different Kat. I ain't got time for no foolishness and I mean that."

"Nell, even if Rock decides to let Tavares make it, how is he going to be able to handle all three of us?" she asked, sounding so sure of herself.

Not gonna lie, but that nigga almost burned my damn nipples off. I still have nightmares and get tingles in my shit just thinking about it. What in the hell do I keep getting myself into with this woman and her sister?

Instantly, a thought hit me. Since she said we were going to get our hands on Tavares, I was going to make him feel the pain he endured upon me.

"Yo Kat, I'll be right back. I have to go do something. Lat, I need to borrow your car for a minute."

"The hell you preach. You're not about to mess my car up," Lat blurted out. I almost turned and punched her in the throat for getting loud with me. Instead, I turned and stared her down until she finally conceded.

"Where are you going Nell? We need to be heading in Tavares' direction in a few to get this over with," Kat sounded out crazily.

"I really don't have time for the back and forth. We can all just go where I need to go, then head to Tavares when I get what I need."

"No, I can't go out until we're going to Tavares. I can't risk being seen. Can't whatever you need to do wait?" Kat pleaded with me. The look of sadness appeared in her eyes, caused me to feel bad for all the pain she'd experienced. It made me feel that I was casting more upon her, but that was not my intention.

"Fine, at least let's swing by your house, so I can grab something. I want to gift Tavares with the same gift that he bestowed upon me," I said, winking my eye at her. The smile that spread across her face let me know that she knew where I was going with this. She nodded her head in agreement as we finished concocting our plan to deal with Tavares, then headed out the door.

By the time I nestled my body in the back seat of the car comfortably, a weird feeling came upon me. I contemplated changing my mind and not going through with any of this, but I couldn't disappoint Kat again. Tonight, was going to end badly, but exactly how bad would it be?

28

T *avares*

When I opened the door, there stood Rock with a sly grin on his face. Snatching him inside the room, I stuck my head out the doorway to peep around the hallway.

"Man, what in the hell are you doing here? How did you find me?" I pondered on that. I know that I only told Drea and Lat where I was staying, so me asking Rock how he found me was a logical question.

"Don't worry about all that. I have ways of finding out anything. I wanted to know where you were, just in case you get in your mind that you want to cross me."

"I'm not even about to go there with you. I told you already that I was done with that shit and you wouldn't have to worry about me going to the cops. The hell I look like going to the cops when I'd have to turn myself in as well?"

"You spit that shit to me now nigga, but all men get ballsy when shit's about to hit the fan. They start throwing shit at you to get you off your game and you start singing like The Temptations."

"Rock, get on with that shit, bruh. I told you that it wasn't going to go down like that. I don't know what other ways you want me to tell you."

"Don't get smart ole bitch made nigga. I hear what you're saying, but I don't believe any of it. How the hell did the police know to go to the warehouse the other day?" That was a good ass question and one I wanted to know the answer to myself.

"Man, I don't know. Why the hell you think I called you when I spotted there was trouble out there? If I really wanted you to get caught, then I never would've said anything to your ass."

Naively, I turned my back on Rock, which was the dumbest move I could've made. The minute I turned my back, he rushed me from behind. Just like a coward to attack someone once they had their back turned. On cue, the door to my hotel room flew open with two John Cena built men flowing through to assist Rock before I could get the upper hand on him.

"Get this nigga. Don't let him get up!" Rock yelled out to his goons. I couldn't believe what the hell was going on. How the hell did this fool find me?

Hands started pummeling on me like a ton of bricks. No matter how hard I fought back, they were getting the best of me. Blow after blow, they were striking my battered body. I was weakening quickly to the point of almost passing out.

Knock... Knock... Knock...

Knocking noises were the next sounds I heard as the men stopped hitting me. Rock placed his hands over my mouth, trying to silence me while one of his goons tried to pull me up. Biting Rock on the hand, "Hellllppppp," I managed to roar.

"Fuck," Rock grimaced, as he hit me in the head with the butt of his gun. My head started spinning and precipitously everything went dark.

⚜

"Who are you and why are you attacking my man?" I could hear a familiar voice ask as I was coming to.

My head was pounding out of control. Trying to open my eyes, the room was still spinning. I could feel liquid running down my face. I wasn't sure if it was blood or tears at this point. It really didn't matter when I realized that I was bound to a chair with my mouth gagged.

When my vision began to clear up, Rock and his two goons were standing before me, and Drea was tied up next to me. But, when the hell did she get there and where the hell was Lat? Her ass should've been here by now. Maybe she would be the person to come in and save us both.

"I'm glad that you finally woke up Tavares. You see that you have company, so at least you won't die alone."

I tried to speak through the gag, but my words were muffled. I was begging for Rock to hear me out because I didn't want to die this way. I didn't deserve to die this way. It didn't make sense what was going on. How the hell dumb could Andrea be to have gotten caught slipping with me? Remind me to tell her the reason she can't ever be on my main team was because she was dumb as hell.

29

ndrea

Finally arriving at the hotel that Tavares was occupying, something seemed off when I reached the outside of his door. When I knocked on the door, I could've sworn that I heard some type of tussle going on inside the room. I tried putting my ear to the door to see if I'd be able to hear anything but when I did, it became quiet.

I knocked on the door again, wondering what was taking him so long to come to answer it if he knew I was supposed to be on my way.

"Hellllppppp!" I heard someone screaming from the inside of the room. The voice sounded like it was Tavares. I wiggled the door handle, trying to get inside. When I got tired of attempting to get in, I made up in my mind that I needed to go get help. Just as I turned to walk away, I was yanked inside the room and hit upside the head. When I came to, I was bound to a chair next to Tavares. His mouth was gagged, but I was able to talk.

"Who are you and why are you attacking my man?" I hysterically asked. I didn't know if I should've been more concerned with what they were going to do to Tavares or what they were going to do to me.

Coming out of his slumber, Tavares began to move around. Blood was dripping from his head and running down his face. He looked like he may've had a concussion and his eyes were super glossy.

"Tavares baby, try to wake up. You can't be sleep or you could die," I tried explaining to him. Now, I'm no nurse, but I know that going to sleep with a concussion could lead to the brain swelling and someone dying. At least, I think I'm right about that.

All I wanted to do was come to the room and get my back blown out by my man, but I ended up being caught up in some shit. Even more reason I should've left Michael's ass alone. I don't know why I always allowed him to get me involved in something stupid. It's not like I come out on top anyways. He's the one that always had something to gain from everything.

Thinking about Michael had me pondering the thought that he was behind all of this. He did threaten to kill me for fear that Kat would be able to identify me to the police and I would end up ratting him out. Even though I told him that wouldn't happen, I knew he didn't believe me and he'd go out of the way to make sure I didn't tell on him.

"Is Michael behind this? Did he send you to kill us?" I heatedly inquired. I knew it had to have been him. What other reason would these thug looking men have to be trying to cause me harm?

"I don't know who a Michael is. But, if it will make you feel better to think he was behind this, then yeah, it was his ass." He started laughing with the two overly large men behind him. I didn't find shit funny. They were about to end my life and I wanted to know why.

Knock... Knock... Knock...

Someone else was knocking at the door. Tavares lifted his head up, as if he was hopeful we were about to be rescued.

"If you scream or try to say anything that'll make the person on the other side of the door suspicious, I'll put a bullet between your eyes. Do you understand?"

Before I thought to open my mouth to speak, all I could do was nod my head in understanding. My body stiffened in complete fear of what was in store for me.

"Go see who's knocking on the door Bruno." The biggest of the three men proceeded to the door. He looked out the peephole and returned to whisper something in the man they refer to as Rock's ear. A wide grin spread across his face as he nodded his head; I assumed to give Bruno the go ahead to answer the door.

My mouth dropped when the door was opened. I couldn't believe who was standing there. They immediately locked eyes with me and squinted their nose up at me. You would've thought they were smelling shit the way their face balled up. What the hell kind of freaky shit are these people involved in?

"What the hell are you doing here?" Instead of a response, I received something so much worse.

🏵 30 🏵

K ateshia
        Rock called me back to let me know that he had Tavares
        in his possession and that there was a woman with him. It
caught me off guard that he would 've had a woman with him when
he'd just invited my sister to come to the room to be with him. What
kind of sick shit did he think was about to go down? I had to wonder
what the hell he was used to doing with Lat and why he thought it
would be okay for him to have her and another woman with him at the
same time. That was another thing I was going to add to the list of
things to ask her about later.

"Why don't you bring him to my house? There's an old shed back
there that we'd be able to do whatever we wanted to him, and nobody
would know?"

"Naw, I can't risk taking him out of here. If him or that bitch
manages to scream, I'll be arrested. I'm not bout to go out behind this
shit," he asserted, which was understandable.

"Aight. I'll just come to you then," I informed him before hanging
the phone up.

"Come on ya'll. We need to get to the hotel."

"Not before we make this stop," Tavares reminded me.

It didn't take Lat no time to pull up in front of the house that I shared with Tavares.

"The spare key is above the doorframe and the passcode is 69187."

"What the fuck kinda code is that?" Darnell looked back at me like I was crazy."

"Just use it nigga and hurry up," I commanded.

Nell got out the car and ran towards the house. Lat and I watched and he located the key and stormed inside.

"Are you sure you want to do this?" Lat probed.

"If I didn't, I wouldn't be talking to your ass right now," I honestly spoke.

By the time she could respond, Nell was running back towards the car with what he needed in his hand. He didn't bother shutting the door behind him and I didn't care enough about anything in that house to make him go back to shut it.

"Let's go," Nell ordered as soon as he was back inside the care.

We rode in silence, all the way to the hotel. I'm sure everyone was thinking the same thing about hoping to get out of this alive. The minute we pulled up in front of the hotel, my heart gained a mind of its own and started uncontrollably pounding.

"You good?" They both asked me.

"Yeah, let's get this shit over with," I boasted trying to sound confident in what we were planning to do.

Wearing a scarf, hat, and sunglasses to hide my identity, we casually walked through the lobby, trying not to be too conspicuous. Standing outside the room door, my palms started to feel sweaty, my heart was still beating fast, my pulse was racing, and beads of sweat were starting to form around my forehead. Why was I so nervous to be going face to face with the monster I once fell in love with?

"Are you okay Kat?" Nell asked, as he softly placed his hands on the small of my back. For some reason, his touch sent a tingling sensation down my spine to my good girl. I knew it was the wrong time to get horny, especially for a man that was breaking other men off, but bear with me; it's been a minute for a sista.

"I'm good. Let's get this over with, so we can get on with our lives."

"Are you going to be able to look at him?" Lat questioned, seemingly concerned about my well-being.

But, being the smart ass that I was, I simply looked at her and said, "I'm as okay with looking at him as I am looking at you. I mean, you are one in the same, right?"

The concern that was once on her face drifted away. I could tell she wanted to bitch slap me, but she was smart enough to know that if she slapped me, her teeth would end up in a pile all over the floor.

"Whatever!" she replied, as she rolled her eyes at me.

"I hope them bitches don't get stuck," I indicated to her as I raised my hand to knock on the door.

The door opened and Bruno was standing there. As we walked into the room, I saw Tavares strapped to a chair with blood dripping on him. Where I used to feel sorry for him, that feeling was no longer there.

"Hey Kateshia," Rock spoke to me, taking me out of my thoughts.

"Hey Rock, how's everything going?"

"They're going mighty good for me. I can't say the same for your punk ass husband though."

"Oh, I'm not worried about him. Hell, that nigga wasn't ever worried about me," I slyly replied. "How's your father?"

"He's doing well. He'll be glad to know that everything with you is well."

"That's good to hear. But, remember that you can't say anything to him until the media announces I'm alive and well. And you can't let him know what part you played in what happens to Tavares."

"Oh, you don't have to worry about that on my end. He doesn't know anything about this side of me and he'll never learn about it from me."

"And he sure as hell won't hear about it from me," I stated as we both started laughing.

"What the hell are you doing here?" I could hear a female voice screech out to me. Out the corner of my eyes, I could slightly see her face.

When I positioned my body where I could make eye contact with her, I was shocked to see it was the person who held me captive.

"How the hell did she end up here? Rock, how did you find the woman that kidnapped me?"

"Huh? I didn't find her. She showed up here to see your deadbeat ass husband."

"So, you did have something to do with me being kidnapped after all," I suggested to Tavares, knowing that I wanted to hurt him right then and there.

Being that his mouth couldn't be used, he kept shaking his head no. I walked over to the female and smacked her across the face without giving it a second thought, calling her a bitch in the process. Smacking her wasn't enough for me, so I took the liberty of backhanding her. Instantly blood was flowing from her nose and her lip was cracked; you could see where her lip was starting to swell. She wailed out in pain, but to me that was nothing compared to the pain I'd endured at the hands of her and her accomplice, Tavares.

"Stupid bitch! Untie me, so you can fight me for real."

"You mean the way I beat your ass when your silly ass let me out that box. You sure you want some more?" I was taunting her now. Could've been because she was tied up; I just didn't feel like fighting.

"Kat, let's get this show on the road; I'm over this," Nell jumped in to say. I side-eyed the hell out of him. Nobody asked him to open his mouth and say shit.

"It's been a pleasure assisting you, Kateshia, but I must get to something a bit more pressing. Tavares, consider this your last day in business with me. Kateshia, make sure you handle him accordingly."

"You definitely don't have to worry about that Rock. Tavares is about to get everything that's coming to him. Please send my regards to your father."

Now, I'm sure you're wondering why I keep bringing up Rock's father. Well, if you can recall, I was signed to a publishing company (Rogers and Rogers Publications) before I got my own. The publishing company that I was signed to, belonged to Rock's father. When I called to throw a wrench in Tavares' plan to meet with Rock, I realized that he was Mr. Roger's son by his voice. The moment I told him who I was, he was game with helping me out, due to the high respect his father had for me. I see now how it pays to not leave places of employment on bad terms.

Rock embraced me into a warm hug before him and his two henchmen walked out the room. I told Nell and Lat to move forward with the next part of our plan. They knew exactly what I meant.

Tavares' eyes got big as hell when Nell hoisted him out of the chair over his shoulder and laid him on the bed. Lat started grabbing corners of the cover, throwing it over to Nell so that they could wrap Tavares in it. While they were doing this, I made my way back to the hallway and grabbed the bat that I sat beside the door and the battery charger that Nell had taken from my house.

"What the hell are you doing?" the woman yelled, questioning what we were about to do to Tavares. I was so tired of hearing her mouth that I grabbed the tape Rock left on the table and placed it across her mouth. I'd rather hear her mumble whatever she was trying to say versus hearing anything come out of her annoying ass mouth.

"It's done Kat. Get him now," Lat stated to me. She didn't have to tell me twice.

I made my way over to where Tavares was bundled up in the covers on the bed and let him have it. Blow after blow, I used the bat to brutally beat him. All the cheating, lying, and abuse I dealt with for years were now moving to the front of my mind, causing me to strike him harder and harder with each blow. The only thing that stopped me was the liquid forming in my eyes. I was about to do the one thing I promised myself I 'd never allow him to make me do again.

Nell walked over to me and cradled me in his arms for comfort. He was the last person I wanted to comfort me, but being in his arms meant a lot; feeling that someone really cared for me was something that I really needed.

"Your turn Nell," I implied to him as I gazed up into his eyes.

Handing Nell the bat, I moved away from the bed. Turning my attention out the window, I tried my best to focus on something else to prevent the tears from falling from my eyes.

🍂 31 🍂

Darnell
　　Staring into Kat's eyes, she gave me the go ahead to get my revenge on Tavares after she'd gotten out the anger and resentment she was harboring against him by beating him with the bat. Maybe we were wrong for handling things the way that we were going about them, but it damn sure was going to feel good.

Strolling back over to the bed, I maneuvered Tavares' body back to the chair he was initially placed in. His body was slumped over. He was drained and weak from all the beatings his body was taking; first, from Rock and his boys, then from Kat. Little did he know, he was not prepared for what I was about to do to him.

Removing the towel from around his body, I looked down at his limped manhood and chuckled to myself. He was working with a nice piece of meat, but nothing that I'd touch. Pulling the battery charger out of the bag I had it placed in, I attached the cables to Tavares; one to his sac and the other to his rod. He moaned out in agonizing pain as the clamps clasped down on his genital area. Still, I felt no remorse. Pressing the button to start the charger, I sent currents through Tavares' body from between his legs. I'd press the button, stop, and then press it again. I did it until I started to smell something that seemed like it was burning.

Inspecting the damages, I saw that the gag that was once covering Tavares' mouth was no longer there. Somehow, he'd managed to move it and now Tavares was crying out for help.

"Make him stop, Kat. I'm sorry for everything I did to you; to both of you," Tavares cried, begging and pleading for his life.

"The pain that you're experiencing now is nowhere near the pain you forced me to endure while we were together. How could you hurt me like that?"

"I don't know. I really don't know. That was never really my intention; I was just more concerned with myself than how you were feeling and I'm sorry."

"You're only saying that because you want me to let you go, but I'm not. The only way you're getting out of here is if you're dead or the police make me release you."

"I'm being sincere in what I'm saying. Kat. Marriage is a challenge, but you should know that there will always be an even bigger struggle. There was always a lot of love between us, but sometimes love just isn't enough. In our case, it wasn't enough, causing me to stray. I apologize for that honestly."

"You say you apologize, but I wanna know why you couldn't let me go. Even if I let you go now, I know that eventually you'll be back."

"If you let me go, this will be it for me. I'll walk away without looking back. I swear!"

"We all know you're just saying that to get her to let you go, but that's not happening. You're going to the police and admit to all your wrongdoings. There's no more escaping for you," I eagerly spat, looking at the fear in his eyes. It didn't faze me at all. In my eyes, this nigga was getting what he deserved.

"Okay, I'll do whatever you want. Just stop torturing me!"

"What are you going to admit to Tavares? Tell me exactly what you're going to own up to when you go to the police," Kat solicited, eyeballing the cables the whole time.

When Tavares realized what Kat was contemplating doing, panic appeared all over his face.

"No Kat, it's me. Tavares! You love me remember? Don't do this," he fearfully implored.

"But Tavares, didn't you love me?"

"Yes!"

"Didn't you lie to me?"

"Yes! And I'm..."

"Ssshhhh... don't try to apologize now. These are yes and no questions. Now, didn't you cheat on me?"

"Kat please," he supplicated, but all his pleas fell on deaf ears.

"YES or NO nigga, simple," she stated, reaching for the cables.

"Yes, I lied, cheated, stole, abused, betrayed, and a whole bunch of other shit to you."

"Good to know that when all the chips have fallen, you can be honest. Now, go ahead and start from the beginning of what happened the night I supposedly went missing. I need to hear exactly what you're going to say to the police."

Tavares opened his mouth, spitting out what really happened that night. He knew he had no other choice but to be honest, especially if he wanted to walk out of this room alive. Andrea sat beside him the whole time attentively listening to every word that lingered from his mouth. Her facial expressions showed pure disgust and hurt from what she was hearing. I knew the hurt look was for what he did to Kat and how she assisted him with hurting her. *Well what do you know, the bitch had a heart after all,* I thought.

"The last thing I want to know is why you had this bald headed, loose pussy, duck feet having, scattered branded, dusty faced-"

"Damn Kat, we get the point that you don't like the bitch. Let's get this over with," Lat whined.

"Fine!" Kat exclaimed with a grin on her face as she walked over to Drea and uppercut the hell out of her, causing both blood and teeth to come flying out her mouth.

Kat then straddled her in the chair and went to work, sending blow after blow to Drea's dome as she tried cry out in agony. The only thing that could be heard coming from her was mumbling.

"Get the fuck off my sister," was the last thing I heard as a shot rang out in the room.

32

ichael

Following Kat to the Barksdale hotel, I had no knowledge of why they would be going there. I saw Kat walk in calling herself disguising who she was, so I immediately knew some shit was about to go down.

As they hopped on the elevator to their desired floor, I watched from the bottom to see what floor they stopped on before I skipped up the stairs two at a time to reach the designated floor. Standing in the hallway, I watched as they proceeded to knock on a room door and was granted access by some big ass dude that I wanted no part of. Once the door was closed, I put my ear to it, trying to eavesdrop to gain as much information as I could. I needed to know what I was up against.

After at least thirty minutes passed with them all being in the room, I saw three men walk out, not closing the door completely behind them. I used that as my time to gain advantage of the situation. I watched on as Kat, Nell, and Lat took turns torturing Tavares. I felt no remorse for him whatsoever. If he wouldn't have hurt Kat so bad, she wouldn't have her brick wall up and I would've been able to get her easily.

From where I was standing, I never realized that there was someone else tied up in the room. It wasn't until I could hear blows being thrown and someone yelping out sounding like a wounded dog that I realized Andrea was the other person they had tied up. When the hell did Kat get bold enough to seek revenge on someone? The thought of her doing something evil only made my dick rock hard. I had to readjust myself in my pants before I could run interference on what was supposed to be going down in the room.

Slowly pushing the door open, it could suddenly be heard making a creaking noise. This caused everyone in the room to turn and look at me. Knowing that I didn't want to cause any real harm to anyone, I had to think of a plan and quick, in order to get both Drea and myself out of there without Kat finding out that I was the one behind most of the things going on with her.

"Get the hell off my sister," I angrily shouted before letting two shots out in the air.

"Michael, what the hell are you doing here?" Kat turned to ask me with the coldest expression I've ever seen on her face.

"I saw you pull up out front, trying to hide yourself as you were getting out the car. I figured you may've been in some type of trouble, so I followed you up here to see if you needed my help. When those three men left, I thought they did something to you, so I rushed in here to make sure that wasn't the case. What the hell is going on in here?"

"Michael, get me out of here!! Don't let her kill me," Andrea shrilled out. The tape that was used to cover her mouth must've fallen off while Kat was beating her ass.

Kat turned to look at her, then looked back at me. I tried to shrug my shoulders, as if I was just as confused as she was. I did my best trying to play as if I didn't know why Andrea was calling out my name.

"Before you ask, she just heard you say my name. That's how she knows who I am," I stated, trying to continuously cover my tracks. I couldn't believe this bitch was about to sell me out in order to save her own ass. But, then again, I knew it was going to happen, which was the reason I told her that I was going to have to kill her ass. I should've stuck to my first mind and took her ass out when I first thought about it.

"Is this true?" Kat questioned Andrea, as if I wasn't standing there.

How the hell could she show her distrust for me in my damn face? After all the shit that I've done for her, this broad had the nerve to question my intentions. She ain't no different than the rest of these bitches I've tried to be down for in the past.

"Michael, you just said get off your sister. What the fuck is going on here?" I'd completely forgot that I announced our relationship when I first walked into the room.

"Damn hoe, I know you just heard me tell you why she said my name. You the same as these other bitches. I don't know why I wasted my time doing all this shit for your ungrateful ass," I soberly returned, still trying to play off the fact that Drea really knew me.

"Excuse me! What did you just say to me?"

"Michael, get me out of this! You're the reason they have me here. I just want to go home like none of this shit ever happened," Andrea stated to me.

"Aight Drea. Go over there and untie her!" I demanded of Kat's twin as I aimed my gun at them.

"What are you doing? Put that damn gun down!" Kat angrily commanded as she began walking towards me.

"If you move any closer to me, I'll blow your damn toes off. I'm done playing these games with your ass. All of you mufuckas are cray as hell if you ask me."

"Yo bro, take that shit down a notch. You not gonna keep calling Kat out her name like that."

"Says the dude that's more of a bitch than she is," I snapped at Darnell. How this ole dick in the booty ass nigga thought he was prepared to step to me beats the hell out of me.

"The fuck did you just say to me?" Darnell returned, as if he was really a match for me.

"Nigga, I suggest you clamp your ass cheeks and mouth together before stepping to me. I guarantee what you think you're getting ain't what you really want!"

That nigga had a lot of nerve thinking I was going to let him come at me like he was King Ding a Ling in this bitch. I was the only one with a gun, so if anybody was going to be walking out alive, I knew for sure it was going to be me.

"Michael, what the hell is going on?" I could hear Kat asking with fear in her voice, as her sister was working to get Andrea untied.

"He's in love with you, Kat, but you continuously played him to the left so he did what he had to do in order to get you where he wanted you. Or at least try to get you where he wanted you. So, he sent me in to get at Tavares and pull him away from you, but your ass just wouldn't die for shit."

Pow... Pow.... Pow...

Three shots to the head sent Andrea drifting back to the floor. Andrea now laid on the floor with her eyes cocked like a pistol with blood draining from her head. She was talking too much. I couldn't let Kat know the extremities I'd really gone through to get her, especially being that none of them panned out.

"Why the hell did you kill her? She was untied. Was it really worth going to jail over?" Kat inquired. She was still trying to inch her way closer to me, as if I was too dumb to see her ass moving.

"I'm not going to jail for murder. You are! Now, shut up and let me think!" I was frantic at this point. Pacing back and forth, there was a big chance I'd burn a hole in the floor.

"Now, I want everyone to sit the hell down before I start shooting. I have an extra clip, so don't think I won't reload and try again if I miss any of you on the first round."

They started scurrying around the room like roaches when I said that I was going to start shooting. Just the way I liked it; people moving at my pace.

33

Kateshia
Grow some balls bitch. You can't go down like this. I started hearing voices telling me to make a move. While it seemed logical to try my best to make Michael think we could be together, my feet were plastered to the floor. There was no way I could move from the spot I was in, for fear that nigga would dead me too. Damn, I hated Lat's ass, but not enough to kill her. There had to be some major bad blood between them for him to just blow his sister's brains out like it was nothing.

"Think man, think. Someone's going to call the police at some point. You've got to get out of here. Not without killing these mother-fuckers first though." Michael was pacing back and forth rambling on and on to himself about something that no one could quite figure out. There were four against one, so surely, we could all take him down. Knowing that what I was about to do could be a bad decision on my part, I knew that I was going to need Tavares.

While Michael continuously moved back and forth throughout the room losing focus on the rest of us, I mouthed to Darnell that I was going to untie Tavares. Darnell looked at me like I'd lost my mind. I'm sure everyone would agree that it could backfire on me, but what else was I to do? True enough, Tavares wanted to kill me, but I also knew that he wouldn't let anyone else do harm to me; it'd only take away from him being able to hurt me.

Easing my way over to Tavares, I could see him slowly trying to come to. I wasn't about to remove the gag from his mouth though; hearing his voice was something I could live without. I hastily removed the tape and rope used to bound him to the chair, then stood back up placing my eyes back on Michael. I had to think of something to get out of, yet, another mess I'd created. How could I be so stupid and not realize that Michael had something to do with what was going on with me? I knew something was off about him when he offered to let me stay with him, but I never thought that he would do something this low.

"Kat," I could hear Lat whispering to me, trying to get my attention. I wanted to look over at her, but at the same time, I didn't need to take my eyes off Michael.

"What girl?" Now was not the time for any of her shenanigans. I was trying to think and she was disturbing me.

"Who the hell is that nigga talking to? You sure do know how to pick them," she stated, trying to be funny.

"Bitch, when you find out, let me know. Something is clearly wrong with his ass."

"Shut the fuck up! Shut the fuck up now! I'm trying to figure out how to get the hell out of this shit. Stop talking to me," Michael aggressively spat. But, who the hell was the nigga talking to? Neither one of us said shit to him.

"Oooooooh..." Tavares began to muffle as his head swung side to side. You would've thought he was drunk if you didn't know that he'd just gotten his ass handed to him. With him making noises, it snapped Michael out of his trance. Luckily, Tavares still appeared to be tied up.

"Shut him up. Don't you see I'm trying to think?"

"I'm sorry Michael. His mouth is already covered; what else do you want me to do?" I seriously asked. It wasn't like there were any other options to keep him quiet.

"Don't worry about it. Since you can't shut him up, I'll do it for you."

Pow... Pow...

Two shots rang out and I could see Tavares' body fall to the floor. Jumping into wife mode, I swiftly ran to his side. I don't care what's happened between us; he was still my husband and I did still care about him. I never wanted to see him dead, just behind bars. Now he was about to die because of me. I'd never be able to live with myself if he died.

"Tavares, please look at me," I begged while smacking his face, trying to get him to open his eyes. I removed the gag from his mouth, trying to give him more breathing room.

"I'm sorry Kat. I'm so sorry," Tavares faintly stated as he began to fade out. I couldn't believe what was happening. This was the kind of shit you expected to see in the movies or on Lifetime; not happening in real life.

"Lat, come help him now," I urgently demanded.

"Hell no! I'm not about to move, so this bastard can try to kill me too. That's your husband so you deal with it."

"Bitch, I didn't ask you; I told you to get down here and help him. You weren't worried about him being my husband when he was plunging his dick inside of you, was you? Now, get your dumb ass down here before I hit you so hard in your throat that you shit out your tonsils." I was scorching hot at the way she responded to me. She had a lot of damn nerves to disobey me, then try to throw this back at me for him being my husband. Now he's my husband? She surely wasn't thinking about the shit when she was fucking him.

"Get your ass up and let's go Kat. You're not about to play me to the left again. We're about to get the hell away from here and start over," Michael strictly commanded. Sirens could be heard coming closer to the hotel. I'm sure someone heard the gunshots and called the police. I was thankful to whoever it was because there was no way I was leaving there with this crazy nigga.

"Ok Michael. I just need to make sure Tavares is going to be okay first," I briefly responded before being jerked up by my arm.

"Aye man, get your hands off her!" I could hear Nell say before Michael pointed the gun at him. Nell threw his hands up in defeat.

Damn, he could've tried a little harder to get Michael to take his hands off me. I think I'm worth a bullet, don't you?

"Lat and Nell, take care of Tavares. I'm going to go with Michael so that you two will at least be safe."

"Oh no, they won't be safe. I'm going to put a bullet in their heads too. The only people walking out of here alive are you and me. I don't care about them and I sure as hell won't be leaving any witnesses."

"But what about the video cameras that saw us all coming in here? Think Michael! There's no way to get out of this. At least make sure Tavares is okay, so you won't have to face two life sentences," I reasoned with him. I could tell that he was thinking about what I said by the way he wrinkled his forehead up.

I was able to get Michael to face me, meaning his back was turned away from Lat and Nell. I continued to talk to him, trying to get him to see how we could make it seem like everything was in self-defense and that Tavares was the one who tried to kill us. Even though I knew I wasn't really going to place the blame of all of this on him, I had to make it believable in Michael's eyes.

Michael was so consumed with what I was saying to him that he apparently forgot Lat and Nell were still in the room. On cue, Nell tackled Michael to the floor. They tussled with the gun for what seemed like forever before another set of gunshots could be heard. I grew frantic, not knowing who was shot. I saw Lat fall to the floor and both Michael and Nell laid dormant where they were once wrestling over the gun. Everything appeared to be happening in slow motion as the door was kicked in and the room was flooded by the police.

34

K*ateshia*
     "Mrs. Jordan, where were you during the time you were declared missing?"

"Mrs. Jordan, do you know who took you from your home?"

"Mrs. Jordan, what happened to your husband?"

Questions were being thrown at me left and right as I was heading inside the police station to make my statement. Everything happened so fast, but all I could think about were the three people who may have been either hanging onto their life or dead all because of me. I never in a million years would've thought that one person could cause so much turmoil in my life.

"Hello Mrs. Jordan, I'm Officer Coleman. I was one of the officers assigned to your case. I'm glad to know that you're okay." She extended her hand to shake mine, but I turned my nose up at her. She may not remember me, but I sure as shit remembered her. She was, yet again, another one of Tavares' many conquests. I wondered if she was really assigned to my case or if she asked to be assigned to it. Hell, I wondered if she and Tavares even remembered each other.

"Thanks Officer Coleman. As you can see, I'm alive and well. I'd like to get this line of questioning underway so that I can check on my family."

"I completely understand that since you've been through so much. The detectives will be in shortly to get your statement."

"Thanks for understanding." That was the only thing I cared to say to her. I hope she didn't think we'd build a friendship.

She led me to an interrogation room. I could clearly see through what was supposed to be a two-sided mirror. Maybe it was supposed to be that way. Regardless, I was ready to get this over with. When the detectives finally arrived, I pulled off my recorder and played back the events from tonight. It was a good thing I remembered to erase everything that happened up until the time that Tavares confessed to everything that he did.

"Is there anything else you'd like to tell us Mrs. Jordan?"

"Anything like what?"

"Like where you were the whole time we've been out looking for you."

"I was taken from my house by the Andrea woman on the day that everything transpired between Tavares, Darnell, and I. She held me inside the old shed on our property. When I got away from her, I went to Michael for help, only for him to turn out to be the one behind most of this mess. Now, if you'll excuse me, I have nothing further to say. I need to get to the hospital."

I could see the detective rolling her eyes at me and I really didn't care. What they wanted to know would have to wait until later. I was more concerned about what happened to the people who risked their lives to protect me.

"I can give you a ride to the hospital if you'd like," Officer Coleman happily stated to me. Normally, I would've told her hell naw, but since I didn't have my purse or anything else on me, I had to take the ride.

Sitting in the back of her patrol car, I felt like I made a bad decision. Each time I looked up, I could see her staring at me in the rearview mirror. One time, it looked as though she was licking her lips. Now, I'm not into that lesbian shit, so she was going to get her feelings hurt if she tried anything funny.

The ride to the hospital was very quiet. I can't remember the last time I was in so much silence. She couldn't pull up to the main entrance fast enough. Without giving her time to come to a complete halt, I jumped out the car and headed inside the hospital. I didn't bother saying goodbye or thank you.

"Hi, I'm looking for my husband, Tavares Jordan," I told the woman at the information desk.

"I don't see his name in our system."

"Please look again. He was shot a few hours ago, and I know they brought him here. He has to be in your system." My mind was moving a mile a minute. Something wasn't right. I then told her to look for my sister's name, Nell's name, or even Michael's name. Someone had to be there. I needed to know what was going on.

"Please have a seat in the waiting area and I'll contact the emergency department to see what I can find out."

I had no choice but to do what she requested if I wanted to find out what I could. I didn't understand how they weren't in the system when I knew that they were all just shot. Well, I don't know if they all were, but I at least knew that Tavares was.

"Hello, Mrs. Jordan, I'm Dr. Sampson." A tall Caucasian male with salt and pepper hair came over to me.

"Hi Dr. Sampson, I'm just trying to find out what's going on. I know that my husband, Tavares, was shot and should've came here, but the lady at the desk was saying that he isn't in the system."

"Mrs. Jordan, I' m sorry to inform you that Mr. Jordan was pronounced dead on arrival." He continued to talk, but nothing that he was saying could be heard. The room started spinning and my body became weak. Standing there was no longer an option for me as the room suddenly grew dark and I passed out.

$$\approx 35 \approx$$

T*avares*

When Kat untied me, I wanted nothing more than to stand up and protect her, but there was nothing I could do. My body was battered and bruised. I couldn't find the strength to do anything. I knew that I put her through more than enough shit to last a lifetime, so being able to stand up for her would've been the best thing I could've done at that moment. Now it's too late.

When Michael shot me, one bullet went through my stomach and the other went through my heart. Kat was so concerned with the fact that I was shot that she never thought to check to see where I was shot at. I don't blame her for that. Even if she would've known where I was shot at, there was nothing she could've done to save me. My life ended the day she walked out my life, so going on without her was no longer an option for me. At least, this way, I could look down on her.

You're probably thinking there was no way I could go to heaven with all the things I've done, right? Well, I hope that's not the case. I knew that I was wrong. That's why I made it a point to ask God for forgiveness while I was taking my last breath.

I allowed my love for control to take over my life, causing me to forget what the most important thing was, which was my marriage, and taking the time to enjoy life. Now, it's time for me to face everything that I've done. I just hope that Kat could make it out of this alive and away from that crazy man.

The last thing I could say to Kat was that I was sorry. I truly meant every word of it, whether others believed me or not. I only needed Kat to believe me. I was just glad that she did stay by my side during my death. The minute she stood up to tell her sister to check on me was the time that I was no more. My soul left my body and I was a happy man. At least this way, I wouldn't be facing any jail time and I could leave this world still married to the woman of my dreams.

❦ 36 ❦

Lateshia

When Michael and Nell were fighting for the gun, I ended up being shot. It went through the front of my shoulder and out the back. I laid on the floor pretending to be dead, just in case Michael ended up coming out on top. One thing I did realize was that Tavares had died before we had a chance to make it out of the hotel room. I was glad I wouldn't have to be the one to break the news to my sister. I couldn't be the same person to break any more bad news to her.

When I got out the hospital, I finally got my test results back and turns out I'm HIV positive. However, I was also pregnant. The thought of taking my own life crossed my mind several times, but then I'd think about my baby and realize that it wasn't worth it. The things I've done wrong to others have finally caught up with me. Now, I was going to have to live my life with a constant reminder of my stupidity.

The one good thing about any of this was that I was going to be someone's mother, which was a prime reason for me to change my life around. People lived with HIV all the time, so there was no reason I wouldn't be able to do it too. I'm looking forward to the chance of starting over and living right. I've even started working to mend the broken relationship I have with both my mother and sister.

Oh, and to let you in on another secret, Tavares is the father of my baby. Yeah, I went back to get another sample of that when all the other mess was going on. Kat didn't know this yet, but what could she do about it? It's in the past and it can't be changed. My only problem now was trying to find a way for my child to be set for the rest of their life by getting some of the money Tavares left behind or even getting part of his company. Either way, I'm going to find a way to make sure that I get mine after all the mess I'd gone through with that man. But, do you think Kat would get mad if I named him Tavares Jr.?

⚜ 37 ⚜

Darnell

Damn, I let Kat put me in another fucked up situation. At least this time would be the last time. I knew she probably thought I died when the gun went off and neither Michael nor I made a move. Nope. The bullet didn't even touch me. I heard that Michael and Tavares both died during the ordeal though. To me, that was the easy way out for them. If you ask me, they both should've been somewhere rotting behind bars. Either way, they couldn't get to Kat again.

After all the questioning by the police and being checked out at the hospital, I could walk away without any criminal charges. I headed to the hotel I was staying in to get my shit and head back to Washington. I prayed all the way there that I'd have a job to return to.

When I made it back, I went straight to HR to talk to them about the events that took place. I was able to keep my job, but it definitely wasn't the same since Cameron decided to quit. The more I thought about it, the more I could see how he really had been down for me since day one. I went to his house trying to see if maybe we could try for a relationship, but he was nowhere to be found. There was a 'For Sale' sign sitting in front of his house, his number had been changed, and he left no forwarding address. Even when I went back to the HR Department to ask for an address to forward some of the things he left in his office, they refused to give it to me.

So, that was that. When I had someone down for me, I pushed them to the side for someone who wasn't really meant to be mine and now I have no one. I guess it's true what they say: you live and you learn. I'm back at square one, which is by my damn self.

❧ 38 ❧

Michael

The police rushed into the hospital room as I was fighting for my life. When we were fighting for the gun and it went off, I ended up being shot in the chest. The police showed up just in time for them to take me to the hospital. I couldn't even pray that things would be okay with me. I didn't want them to be. There was no way I could live in this world knowing that I'd killed my sister and probably others for someone who never wanted me and probably would've never been with me, even if I did do things the right way and waited for her to make the decision on her own to be with me.

Truthfully, I probably would've taken my own life if I didn't die at the hands of someone else. I needed to rid myself of all the demons I'd been facing for most of my life. Now, I no longer have to worry about any of those things. I didn't bother asking for forgiveness because there was no need to. To me, it made no sense to do something and ask for forgiveness, only to continue to do it again. Each time I did something wrong in regards to Kat or someone else, I made it a point to ask for forgiveness, but I'm sure I was all out of times to be forgiven for doing the same thing. At some point, it's like you're doing it just because and I definitely didn't want to be that person.

I didn't end up with Kat, but neither did Tavares. That was all that I really wanted in the end, if I couldn't have her. Coding on the operating table, I ended up dying.

❦ 39 ❦

K*ateshia*
Over the last year or so, I've been through some unbeliev-able shit. I wouldn't wish any of it on my worst enemy. When the doctor told me that Tavares was dead, I lost it. I can't lie and say that I didn't love him because I did. I just wasn't in love with him anymore. He'd done too much for me to continue to stick around with him.

In the end, I did manage to come out on top from the relationship though. I got everything that he owned after his death. I sold the house, any property in his name (including his law firm), and the cars. When I heard from the insurance company, I collected that money and bounced from New York.

Darnell and I never spoke again, which was for the best. He was more into ass than I thought, if you get my drift. Lateshia was walking around pregnant with what I presumed to be Tavares's baby, even though she'll never confirm that. I couldn't care less though because he's dead and gone. Anything he used to have was no longer his. It all belonged to me and the minute that she comes trying to get it, she'll have hell to walk through trying to convince the courts that it was his baby. Even still, she wouldn't get shit because everything in his will indicated it was to come to me. Now, the only thing I would give her, was $2 for the hoe she was.

Don't turn your nose up at me. That was my husband that she slept with. If she wanted anything from this, she should've gotten it from him before I cremated his ass. Guess she can ask him when she gets to hell why he didn't think about her when he was making his will out? Yes, I know the baby is innocent, and so am I. She better figure that shit out herself.

With all the money I was sitting on, I was able to start my life over without telling anybody where the hell I was.

CPSIA information can be obtained
at www.ICGtesting.com
Printed in the USA
LVHW08s0000220818
587523LV00015BB/1517/P